THE VIRGINIA GHOST MURDERS

by

Leslie Raymond Sachs

Pussycat Press
Richmond, Virginia
1998

Pussycat Press
Fax (804) 755-1880
THE VIRGINIA GHOST MURDERS
ISBN 0-9663363-4-8

© 1998 by Leslie Raymond Sachs
Published by:
Pussycat Press
Post Office Box 9575
Richmond, Virginia 23228-0575
Voice (804) 755-6118
Fax (804) 755-1880
pssyctpr@ix.netcom.com

Printed in the United States of America
First Printing September 1998
5 4 3 2

THE VIRGINIA GHOST MURDERS is registered with the Writers Guild of America, East.

Sachs, Leslie Raymond
  The Virginia ghost murders / by Leslie Raymond
Sachs.

  ISBN 0-9663363-4-8
  Library of Congress Catalog No.: 98-85047

"A murder mystery with a different twist, Sachs keeps the reader spellbound with his interweaving of ghosts and reality . . . an easy, flowing style that is pleasant to read".
- Covington *Virginian Review*

An Amanda Poe Mystery

A trio of murdered young women. A forgotten and haunted old mansion. And a riddle that reaches back in time to the origins of the Old Confederacy.

We find death in a Southern setting in THE VIRGINIA GHOST MURDERS, which introduces us to the mysterious and beautiful investigator Amanda Poe. Amanda is descended from the famous Edgar Allan Poe, and she has a knack for cases where the trail of murder leads down strange and eerie pathways.

Steeped in the blemished history of the Old South, and tinged with echoes of the supernatural, THE VIRGINIA GHOST MURDERS is a remarkable book that actually invents a spooky new category of detective writing. Fresh and brilliant, it has become an instant classic of the American mystery genre.

About the Author

Leslie Raymond Sachs is an intriguing and unique contemporary writer, well known for a nonfiction investigation of the auto industry (Signet/Penguin Putnam) that has been called the best book ever written on the topic. He is a graduate of Harvard and The City University of New York, holds a Master's degree in philosophy, and is an award-winning former employee of the United States Department of Justice.

He lives in old Rebel territory in central Virginia, within an easy drive of both the Blue Ridge mountains and the Chesapeake Bay.

The author may be contacted at:
lesliers@juno.com

Angel in Black

The first time I saw Amanda Poe she had drawn her gun and was ready to shoot. I could tell that she knew how to handle a pistol. And I could see that she was beautiful.

It was almost twilight. I had been walking home toward my townhouse, in the ancient residential neighborhood of Richmond, Virginia that is called Church Hill. I was at the corner of 24th and Franklin, about a block from the famous St. John's Episcopal Church where Patrick Henry had urged the Colonial rebels to "Give me liberty or give me death!" And now, more than two hundred years later, it was *me* who was looking death in the eye as the bells of St. John's rang the six-o'-clock chime.

1

My name is David Allan. I'm a private detective and I always carry a gun, partly because of my work and partly because I live on the edge of a crummy neighborhood. My work up to now had not been glamorous: Naughty wives and husbands, insurance fraud scams, the usual low-paying detective nonsense. But in a few seconds I would be in the first gunfight of my life.

Thirty yards ahead of me on the sidewalk there was a young woman of college age, strolling along at an easy pace. As she got to the corner, a car on the cross street slowed down just in front of her. Deep inside of me the warning bells rang: something terrible was in the works.

I began to have the sensations that cops and other detectives told me they had felt in situations of deadly danger. Time slows down. Your hearing begins to disappear. You see reality in a tunnel, it's just you and the situation in front of you. And so it was for me, in that moment, as my heart began pounding.

The car on the cross street coasted to a halt. Its passenger side door opened sharply in front of the young woman. She stood at the corner, stunned and not moving, as the two hoodlums in the car looked her over. The air was thick with menace and evil.

I knew that two other young women from Richmond had been raped and murdered in recent weeks, their bodies dumped out on country roads nearly forty miles away. It was possible the killers of those women were in front of me now.

I reached into my jacket to draw my pistol, and I tried to quicken my pace forward. But my legs and my gun hand all seemed bound and cramped in their motion, like in a nightmare where you are trying to run and yet you can barely move at all.

As slowly as I seemed to be drawing my gun, however, the scene in front of me was locked in an even slower time-crawl, like a videotape moving only one frame per second. While I raised my pistol, a scuzzy-looking guy came out of the car and spoke to the young woman. I could not hear his words. He held a shiny silver revolver in his right hand, and with his gun he motioned the girl into the vehicle.

She raised her hand to her mouth to stifle her own scream.

"Hey!" I shouted. My voice seemed to echo forever along the Franklin Street brownstones, like a hiker's call in a canyon. My arms and legs were still as if weighed down by unseen forces; I felt as if I was living in a slow-motion movie. My pistol was coming up into position, but it wasn't quite on target yet.

The bad guy with the silver revolver hadn't noticed me before, but suddenly he knew that I was there. The guy's lips formed an obscenity and he began to point his gun up toward *me*. My body electrified with energy.

I was fifteen yards away, a little bit of a long shot. I had practiced a lot on the target range, but I had never fired a gun at a person in my entire life. Now, though, it was shooting for real. It would be death for either him or me. A dozen years of range habits took over as I leveled my gun on the bad guy. The three white dots on my pistol's sights lined up on the man's chest. I felt a rush of satisfaction as I realized I would win. His gun was still canted wildly in his hand. He didn't have a prayer, but he probably wasn't the praying type.

I felt my gun's blast, I saw the flash, but I did not hear the sound. The silver-tipped hollowpoint bullet from my pistol's firing chamber hit the man just under his throat. He crumpled and fell like a sack of potatoes falling off a truck. I learned then that when you see someone get shot to death in real life, it is different from television or the movies. Actors fall more gradually. People who are shot for real just *drop*, helplessly and suddenly, limbs all a-jumble. It's a graceless and sickening sight.

As the bad guy fell, the young woman in front of me who was his intended victim remained frozen and motionless, even though the bullet from my gun had whizzed by just inches away from her. Out of the corner of my eye I sensed that a second woman was across the street, but my instincts told me this other woman was a harmless passer-by.

In front of me, however, another threat emerged. The driver of the car reached under the seat for a sawed-off shotgun. I saw the double barrel coming up, but he wasn't quick enough. Like his partner whom I'd just shot, the driver didn't get a chance to pull *his* trigger, either.

My front sight leveled on his cheekbone and so, with the second bullet from my gun, I blew his face apart. What was left of his head fell on the steering wheel and turned on the car's horn. It was a mess. His dead foot was still jammed on the brake pedal.

My vision began to widen. I could hear ringing in my ears, and the running motor in the hoodlums' car. The young woman I had saved, who'd just seen two men get shot to death in front of her, screamed and then started to cry. My cocked pistol was still pointing forward. I looked around and to the side of me and then I saw something else astonishing.

A beautiful dark-haired woman stood almost parallel to me, just across the narrow street in front of a parked car. She was anchored, one leg forward, in a classic shooter's stance, her slit skirt revealing a leg adorned in dark pantyhose. In her hands was a black compact pistol, pointed toward the bad guys whom I had just shot. She looked at me and smiled gently. "I think you got 'em!" she said.

I had just met Amanda Poe.

* * *

I had thought I was alone in that gunfight, and so it was comforting to find that in the moment of truth an angel had been there backing me up all along. Although I had done the shooting, Amanda had been ready to put her life on the line along with mine. It turned out she was also a private detective who lived in the neighborhood.

The cops came quickly, and an ambulance right afterwards. The two hoodlums I had shot were already dead. I'd always bought premium ultra-deadly ammo for carrying in my pistol. The $16.95 for a small box of twenty cartridges no longer seemed expensive now that these pricey bullets had saved my life.

The young, stunned woman whom I had rescued from the creeps in the car was comforted by the medics on the scene. She was okay but obviously shook up. Sobbing and crying every little while, she went down to the police station with the rest of us. She was safe now, but I knew she would live forever with the image of two men being shot to death right under her nose.

Amanda Poe, on the other hand, was very cool and didn't appear razzled by what she had witnessed. "That was *really* good shooting," she said as we rode together to police headquarters, just as if I'd scored some 10s on paper targets. Then she added, with sweet concern, "You're okay, aren't you?"

"I think so," I replied. But I wasn't sure yet if I really *was* okay. After all, I had just killed two people, and I felt strange. However, I didn't feel any regret or depression. Instead, I guiltily felt thrilled and proud, like when I made the big pass at a high school football game.

I had always read that cops and soldiers and detectives can suffer emotionally after they shoot somebody, even when the circumstances completely justify the use of deadly force. I also read that some people who killed bad guys could take it almost in stride. I was curious to see how I would turn out. Maybe, I thought, it would all affect me later, and I would wake up in the night screaming. But for now, I actually felt a little smug.

As we rode to police headquarters, the attractive Amanda Poe was sitting next to me in the back of the police cruiser, her skirt parting and once again giving me a view of her well-toned thigh. *What a nice looking woman,* I thought. She had looked so perfect there on the street, with her gun in her hand, legs apart, feet solidly planted, long dark hair cascading onto her shoulders. She had been as ready to shoot as I was. She was my kind of woman – beautiful and capable.

I fantasized about making love with her, kissing her dark red lips and caressing her lovely limbs. And then I thought: Geez, I had just killed two people less than half an hour before, and here I was, already indulging in typical male sexual reverie.

"You shot so fast," said Amanda. "I was just half a second behind you on the draw, and I couldn't see straight into their car from that angle across the street. And you were great, you didn't even blink. That girl you saved really owes you – What's the old custom, you save someone's life and then she becomes your slave, isn't that it?"

I smiled. Amanda didn't say anything else. She put her hand on my leg for a few seconds, to let me know she appreciated what I did and what I must be feeling. I looked out the car window at the darkened Richmond streets just outside of the main police station. Rarely had I felt so vividly alive as I did in this moment, sitting with a beautiful woman right after a gunfight.

I had faced the moment of truth and won. Guns had been drawn, people were ready to kill, and *I* had emerged victorious. It is a feeling that can be fully understood only by those who have shared the gunfight experience. I was a successful modern gladiator, and I felt as if the police cruiser was a chariot of triumph.

We got to the station and it was about three hours of questioning and the expected bureaucratic bullshit. I knew the routine, because I'd been a cop myself in Chesterfield county, the suburban area south of Richmond city. Because of the gunfight, news reporters were hanging around the station, and there was a lot of talk about how the two scuzballs I had shot were probably the killers of the two recently murdered young women. I made a brief statement to the camera about how I was glad to help a young woman in trouble, and beyond that I didn't have anything more to say. Reporters tend to ask a lot of stupid questions about gunfights, and so I didn't want to waste time with them.

The cops pulled the rap sheet on the corpses, and sure enough they were scum: auto theft, assault, drug arrests. But it didn't add up to me that they had killed the two women previously. Their profile was two-bit criminal trivia, not the sustained psychosis that makes a real slasher. My instinct was that these guys I had shot were just car crawling joyriders, that it was a spur of the moment thing, and that they hadn't killed anyone before they tried to kill me. I felt that I ought to know, considering as how I had shot these bad guys myself. I felt connected to their departed spirits, as if our gunfight together joined me and the dead hoodlums in some sort of deranged and perverted kinship.

The Richmond authorities were pretty good about the shooting. About nine o'clock the district attorney announced to the press that I was in the clear, that no charges would be brought, and that I was a licensed private detective in a "righteous shoot" as cops called it. They fired my pistol twice more in the lab to get some ballistics, but they even gave me my gun back. I still had eleven bullets, which was more than enough for any trouble I might encounter on the way home.

The young woman whom I'd saved from getting kidnapped and probably raped, she remained in an upset state. Her sister drove in from the suburbs to collect her. She kept on mumbling about what a mess it was when the bad guy's face got blown out in front of her, and I could appreciate that it was not a pretty sight. I realized afterwards that neither she nor her family ever thanked me for saving her from a terrible fate. To them, I was just another piece of scenery in an unpleasant situation they'd rather forget. Such a cold lack of thanks irritates me. But that's life.

Amanda Poe, on the other hand, was a very comforting presence to me that evening. Although she'd never been a cop herself, she made me feel as if she was someone I could rely on in a sticky situation. When the police released us both, she invited me to her home.

"Come on over to my place," she said, "I've got some great tea."

"Yeah, okay," I grunted. I'm not always eloquent.

* * *

We got to Amanda's place, the upper floor of a townhouse about two blocks from where I live, close to the high-crime area. There were bars on her windows, but inside it was cozy. And the tea was good.

We talked shop for a while, about detective work and how tacky and mundane most of the jobs were, and how some of the clients didn't pay on time.

We talked about how I had been a cop for three years. There was no special reason why I had quit, other than I didn't like all the bureaucratic rules and structure that are part of being a cop on a modern police force. I prefer being more independent, even though I had made less money as a private detective. Amanda nodded because she understood. She seemed to be the independent type, too.

I asked her why she had become a detective. "A lot of reasons," she replied. "Adventure. A sense of mystery. And I think I even enjoy being in danger."

I was startled. I wasn't used to this kind of thinking expressed by a woman's voice. Here we were, a few hours after a shooting death which we both had seen, and Amanda was completely comfortable with herself. And she seemed comfortable with me even though I had done the killing. It was something I would see more and more in Amanda, that she was on familiar terms with death and with the darker sides of existence.

We talked about topics that grew closer to that of the shooting. We talked about guns. She carried a compact 8-shot Ladysmith, a Smith & Wesson pistol with a smoother mechanism designed for women. I carried a bigger 15-shot

Ruger. We both preferred dark guns for street carry, and we both used the same kind of ammo, super high-velocity hollow points. These bullets had killed two men this evening.

"That ammo worked just like the advertising promised," I commented. It was the first time we'd talked directly about the shooting since leaving the police station.

Amanda nodded her assent. She said nothing, but looked at me with an expression that was both profound and sweet. All of a sudden I felt a surge of emotion. For the first time that evening, I felt a residue of fear and vulnerability.

I accepted the chance of looking stupid, but I did what my heart wanted. I stood up, walked over to Amanda, and put my head on her shoulder. Surprising even myself, I shed a few tears and sobbed briefly. Amanda hugged me, knowing exactly the comfort I needed. Her black cotton top was damp at the shoulder from my brief blubbering. And then my tears stopped, as suddenly as they had started. In that moment I knew for sure that, shootings and all considered, I would be fine. I was a survivor.

Amanda kissed me on the cheek, a magically comforting kiss, and then hugged me again. "You were *wonderful*," she said, in a tone that suggested that I was a hero. "I admire a man who's strong enough to cry," she added. And then she brought me some more tea.

Later she asked, "Would you please sleep on my sofa tonight?" I didn't know if that was for my benefit or hers, but it felt good to share a home with another human being that evening. She brought me a blanket and pillows, and she touched my shoulders fondly before she herself went to bed. I put my loaded pistol under the sofa and looked around the dark apartment, now lit only by the glow from the moon and stars coming in through the windows.

I felt good there at Amanda's. It had been a significant day in my life. I had killed. Righteously and lawfully, yes, but I was now and forevermore a man who had taken the life of another human being, in fact, two human beings. I was older and a little wiser, more mature in my outlook on the world. I would never be truly innocent again, having taken other people's lives. But here in Amanda's apartment, with her brown-and-black cat watching me go to sleep, I felt at peace, temporarily sharing a home with a woman who was obviously unique and special.

I looked around my dim and dark surroundings. Above the doorway into Amanda's apartment I saw there was a pedestal with a large and ominous bust of a bird, a bird who seemed to be staring at me in the darkness. It was, I realized, the bust of a *raven*. Amanda *Poe* was my hostess' name, and I smiled to myself as I remembered the lines of the famous poem:

> *Once upon a midnight dreary*
> *While I pondered, weak and weary...*

My own last name is connected as well with the author of *The Raven*. My last name, Allan, is spelled the same as that of the family who had adopted the orphan Edgar Poe and gave him his middle moniker. And now, here we were all together, the raven, Allan, and Poe. A poetic confluence in a night of death.

I put my hand on my pistol once more. This cold metal item was a tool which had saved my own life and the dignity of a young woman.

The weapon felt good in my hand. I could still smell the gunpowder from when it had been fired. I put the gun back on the floor.

With Amanda's cat keeping watch, I fell into a deep, heavy sleep. In the morning I knew I had dreamed serious dreams but I could not remember any of them.

* * *

I awoke to see Amanda making breakfast for us. She was wearing a flannel nightgown with lace frills. She looked like a wise little girl.

"Quoth the raven, Good morning," I said. "Tell me, are you a descendent of Edgar Allan Poe? I didn't think he had any."

"It's too soon for you to know all my secrets," she replied. She was smiling and beautiful. A lot of women look attractive in the evening, but I've found that any woman whom I really like appeals to me in the morning, too. And Amanda Poe in her bedclothes looked delicious enough to have for breakfast.

"You've got a name in the raven's family tree, too," Amanda continued. "It was a Mr.

Allan who gave his adopted son Edgar Poe the childhood beatings that made him so brooding and sensitive. Is there a family connection, Mr. David Allan?"

"My family's from near Roanoke, in the Virginia mountains," I said. "I disavow any knowledge of abuse possibly committed by my distant ancestors against the author of *The Raven*. I'm sure my grandfather would have bragged about any connection with Edgar Allan Poe, even if Edgar's stepfather Allan was a pervert. But I can't say for sure there's not some distant relation between my lineage and the Allans of Edgar Allan Poe."

"So we might have mutual secrets to explore," Amanda responded, with an impish twinkle.

I didn't know what to say. I did want to share some secret moments with Amanda, but I didn't want to appear crude and forward with a woman I so respected.

We shared sausage and eggs and muffins and then I said good-bye, shaking her hand on my departure. As is typical among private snoops, we promised to share any future detective work that required a second fiddle. As I walked down the street away from Amanda's place, I wondered just how soon I would be able to ask her for a date. I fussed mentally over the issue of, How do you ask for a date from a woman who had watched you shoot two people to death?

But Amanda and I would meet soon enough, and we would once again face danger side by side. And I would discover that Amanda Poe was a woman of depth and secret power unlike anyone I had ever known.

Old Southern Money

As it turned out, I didn't have to figure out a way to ask Amanda Poe for a date. She called me.

About ten days after the shootout, I was sitting at home in the morning, browsing through the newspaper and wondering how I was going to pay my bills. I was slowly facing the fact that I might have to apply for an hourly job as a security guard to tide me over the season's lull in the detective business. It was almost summer – hot and sticky in Richmond – when clients tend to go on vacation and take their money with them.

The front page of the paper had a story about another young woman murdered. She had been raped and slashed horribly, and then

21

dumped on the same back road in Louisa county that had received the bodies of two other victims in the months before.

This new murder proved that my instinct was right about the two men I had shot. The creeps I popped on a Church Hill street were not the serial ladykillers as the newspapers and some of the cops had assumed. With this latest murder, it was clear that whoever had killed those first two women was still on the loose.

A third young woman was now dead, after spending her final hours in a nightmare of rape and horror. It was probable there would be more victims before the dragnet closed in.

I fantasized about finding that killer and shooting him dead. I knew now what it was like to kill a bad guy, and although it was an unsettling experience I knew I could pull the trigger again given an appropriate opportunity.

Deep into my fourth cup of coffee, thinking about my empty refrigerator and empty wallet and empty client docket, my life was suddenly changed when the phone rang. It was Amanda Poe.

"David!" she said, her tone warm and positive. "I've been *thinking* about you," she continued, intriguingly. "How are you?"

"A little bored, but otherwise good," I replied. This was not quite true. I was not just bored, I was broke. "It's nice to hear from you," I added. "I've wanted to call you but I wasn't sure after what we went through together."

"I understand, but it's all right," she said, encouragingly. "Anyway, would you be free for a job?"

A job! Money! Maybe enough to pay the bills and take Amanda out on a nice date. This *was* good news.

"Yes, I am," I said, trying not to sound too excited. "Are you sure there's room for me?"

"Oh, yes, definitely," she answered. "Top pay, too." She definitely had all my attention. Amanda continued: "Can you meet me this afternoon, about quarter of two?"

"Where?"

"By the sculpture in front of the Federal Reserve building, at the entrance to the Money Museum."

"Sure," I said. "Where are we going?"

"To meet a very distinguished client. Dress nice," she suggested.

"That may be a bit beyond me," I said. I hadn't bought a new suit or sportcoat in three years.

"Don't worry, as nice as you can, that'll be fine. I think we can get cash up front, too."

"You're an angel," I said.

"Not always," she replied. We both laughed and said good-bye.

* * *

I got there early and took a few minutes to tour the small Money Museum on the ground floor of the Federal Reserve tower. I looked over exhibits such as a huge bar of gold and $100,000-denominated paper currency, displays which have a particular fascination for the broke and the near-broke. After gawking at the kind of wealth I would never possess, I walked back out into the sunshine to wait for Amanda.

Outside of the Federal Reserve building there is a large, goofy metal sculpture composed of waving wands of steel that clang together like a huge wind chime. It's a vaguely irritating sound that keeps bums from loitering in the area, but today this sound of metal bouncing on metal seemed chilling and morbid to me, like the sound of a jail cell door closing, or the sound of a lid thudding shut on a metal coffin.

Above me, birds were flying, seabirds that had flown up the path of the James River which winds through Richmond. They seemed a sign of life; the clanging metal, the opposing symbol of death. I thought about another item of metal, the gun in my holster, and how I had used that gun with fatal effects less than two weeks earlier. I had shot two men dead, on a day just as nice as this one.

The sun was shining now but my mood was dark. And into that dark mood there suddenly appeared Amanda Poe.

She was attired in a deep blue suit and heels with no blouse, and her jacket parted slightly to give a glimpse of the black bra she was wearing. She seemed even more beautiful than when I first saw her. I still had a sense of brooding and darkness, but Amanda seemed to draw me to her with an eerie, murky sexiness that could make even the face of death seem alluring.

As we talked and strolled along together, it seemed to me we were a very powerful pair. Two people with concealed weapons, looking like ordinary pedestrians beneath the afternoon sun in downtown Richmond. We had a lot in store for ourselves in the near future.

We walked together about two blocks, to an old three story building that had been lavishly maintained inside of a walled garden and iron gates. It was the private headquarters of the Horton family conglomerate. The Hortons were one of the oldest wealthy Richmond families that had originally made money in slaves and tobacco, and now they had a quiet multimillion dollar holding company for real estate and other businesses.

Anyone working at the Horton headquarters would obviously be a significant client for us. I did not realize as we went through the front gate that we were on our way to meet Dabney Horton himself. We were ushered directly to the office of this patriarch of the Horton family, whose first name of Dabney was shared with many other Dabney Hortons before him.

The most famous Dabney Horton was Colonel Horton during the Civil War, who led a curious attack on behalf of the Confederacy that is not well known in the North. It took place during the last siege of Petersburg, a city about forty miles south of Richmond.

One day during that siege, in the space of a few hours before dawn, Colonel Horton assembled one of the most remarkable attack formations ever seen during the War Between the States. In the camps at Petersburg, the Southern troops included several companies of black soldiers. Remarkably, there were indeed a few hard-fighting units of black soldiers who batted *for* the Confederacy during the Civil War. Some of them were slaves, some of them were freemen, but they did remain largely loyal to the South even after the Emancipation Proclamation.

In preparing for a brave and bold attack that nearly broke the Union lines, the Colonel Horton of 1864 assembled a tactical unit of some 400 of the best troops he could find among the throng of hungry rebels camped at Petersburg. Of those 400, more than 250 were black. So, in those last desperate months of the Civil War, out of purely tactical considerations, the Confederate Colonel Horton put together in one night the only fully integrated combat fighting unit seen by either side in the War.

Just after dawn one summer day, Colonel Horton and his 400 Confederate troops, with 250 black faces among them, led a screaming charge against Union lines. The Northern soldiers were stunned: Since they saw themselves as the liberators of slaves, they were shocked and nearly overwhelmed by seeing hundreds of black faces in Rebel uniforms charging up the hill to kill them.

Today, some Southerners look at Colonel Horton's charge as the finest hour of the Old South, when blacks and whites fought and died together on terms of complete equality. And die they did; the charge punched the Union lines, but as the Union troops finally collected their wits and senses they shot down all 400 of the integrated unit. Only about two dozen survived,

Colonel Horton – himself shot three times – miraculously among them, wounded in both an arm and a leg.

It is a story that is not written in histories of the Civil War, because the image of blacks fighting to the death for the Old South is a hard one to justify and explain. But in old Virginia and other parts of the South, Colonel Dabney Horton's courageous but failed charge up the hill at Petersburg is a tale that is still told with interest and awe.

* * *

The Dabney Horton with whom Amanda and I were meeting, is a direct descendant of the Colonel Dabney Horton of the Civil War. That Colonel, after recovering from his battle wounds, continued the family's successful business enterprises in the late 1800s, and much of the land owned by the historic Colonel Horton is still in Horton family hands today.

The modern Dabney Horton's office has a beautiful view of the still wild-running James River. Upon entering I was impressed with just how expensive and luxurious an office can be: The oriental rugs, the hand-carved furniture, the gold-edged writing instruments. All of Horton's surroundings were simply exquisite.

He greeted Amanda warmly and personally, and was quite cordial to me. He was clearly a true Southern gentleman, with that elegant, slightly rolling classic Richmond accent. He spent a minute concluding business with his secretary before giving full attention to us.

For a while he and Amanda made small talk, and I gathered that Amanda and his wife were friendly acquaintances and shared membership in the Daughters of the Confederacy. Horton explained to me that he had already seen the extent of Amanda's abilities in locating a very precious document that had saved another family's inheritance. Through some kind of mystical intuition that Amanda did not reveal to him, she was able to find the hiding place on an old estate where documents had been buried in 1862.

"You see, Mr. Allan," said Horton, "a number of us are aware that Miss Poe is an unusual woman who can do things that no one else can accomplish. We don't know her secrets, but we know she's someone we can trust. She's spoken very highly of you as someone of immense abilities, and on that basis I'd like to offer both of you a task of great importance to the citizens of this Commonwealth."

I was surprised that Amanda felt she knew me well enough to recommend me for a job with the likes of Dabney Horton. Amanda had seen me kill two bad guys and spent an evening with me, and on that basis she was bringing me into trusted contact with the high and the mighty. I was flabbergasted, but I had not yet appreciated the power of Amanda's intuitions.

"Now to discuss my proposed project for you two," said Horton. "You know those three young Virginia ladies who've been murdered these recent weeks?"

I nodded.

"The *killer*," said Horton, with a tone of disgust spilling into his elegant Southern diction, "The killer is who I'd like you two to find for me."

* * *

"The police are at dead ends on this," explained Horton. "They've done their job, gone all the usual routes. But there's nothing turning up. The FBI's also in on it, with a serial killer on the loose, but the guess is that it's going to be a long time before even they can uncover something, and by then two or three or four more young women might be dead.

"I have contacts in the state police, in Louisa county, and here in Richmond who will, confidentially, keep you up to date on anything they find. I'm hoping that, by pursuing your own avenues of investigation parallel to the police, you might find something or somebody they can't.

"Do anything you want, use anything you need. I'll give each of you $3000 per month plus all expenses, and $25,000 each if you get lucky and catch our man. The resources of the Horton family are entirely at your disposal. Here are my phone numbers, contact me anytime of day or night. Don't ever be afraid to disturb me. I only ask one thing: If you find out something, or have a lead on someone, *tell me first*. Tell *me*, even before the authorities! I work with them very closely, but sometimes I can personally touch matters with an extra effectiveness. Please – your promise – *tell me first*. Is that acceptable?"

I nodded and so did Amanda.

"Here are the names of my contacts with the law enforcement people. They're a good place to start, with all the information about the case. Mention my name and they will give you anything you need. You will have identification supplied to you as temporary special investigators deputized by the state police, but please keep your profile discreet.

"This is an important personal matter to me. I want this evildoer bound over to justice. I *want him*, I absolutely do. Here's a start on your money, with some for expenses -- $5000 each." The money was in brown envelopes, and it was cash. I pocketed mine gratefully. Amanda's disappeared into her purse.

"Anything more I can tell you now?" asked Horton.

"Yes," I said. "Why?"

"Why?" repeated Horton.

"Yes," I said. "Why are you doing this? Why the special interest in this murderer?"

"That's complex," said Horton, sounding honest. "I have a daughter at the university here in town, and, as you probably know, two of the young women murdered were also students there, and were about the same age.

"Two of the murdered women were black, and I think there's some racial element in these killings. I find that offensive.

"My family has always had a civic concern for the citizens of this Commonwealth. If my family can see a special way to help, my impulse is to take that route and see what can be done beyond the usual channels.

"Finally, the places where the bodies were left – the back roads of Louisa county – is where my family owned land more than a hundred years ago. That area today is home to black families of modest means, good people who are descended from slaves my family owned before 1863. The guilt of slaveowning does not die in a Southern family, there's a sense of responsibility that remains. I am sure that none of the people on that road have anything to do with this crime, and I want to relieve them of this horror and this burden. Although it is more than a hundred and thirty years since *my* ancestors owned and abused *their* ancestors, I still feel responsible. I don't mind spending money to help stop these crimes so those good country people can be left in peace.

"I hope that's enough to make you understand," he concluded.

I nodded.

Our business finished, we made small talk for a little while and then we said good-bye. Amanda had been fairly quiet, and I gathered that actually the whole affair had been arranged in advance between herself and Horton.

Before we left, Horton reiterated again: "Remember, call me. Anytime, day or night, call me first, even four a.m. is fine. I want to always be the first to know."

"We'll call," I promised.

* * *

As we left the building, I thanked Amanda for letting me in on this job. That $5,000 newly in my pocket had just saved my financial behind.

"I'm really amazed you thought of me for joining you in this," I told her. "I'm not really any kind of spectacular detective. I'm fast with a pistol, but I'm not Sherlock Holmes."

"You're good," said Amanda with assurance. "I know you better than you think."

"Should I be scared of that?" I said with a grin.

Amanda smiled. "By the way," she asked, "What did you think of Dabney?"

"I liked him," I said. "But I don't really understand what it's like to be that rich or that powerful."

"Like everything else, it's a burden," said Amanda, soberly. I nodded, but I only half understood. Having all that money, I thought, would be nice. I wouldn't object to being rich.

Amanda and I said good-bye to each other across the street from the Federal Reserve building where we had met. "We've got work to do now, don't we?" I asked.

"Pick me up at nine tomorrow morning?" asked Amanda in reply.

"Nine sharp, right," I said. As she got into her small black car, I found myself wishing we were not occupied together in such serious, murderous business. I found myself wishing for a reason and circumstance in which I could kiss Amanda's delicate lips. Perhaps, I hoped, our work together would later give me an opportunity to have that kiss.

Voices at the Morgue

    The first task for Amanda and myself was to learn whatever information had been gathered by the authorities in their own work on the murders. We went to the state police headquarters in south Richmond, where we met with a deputy chief who was a contact of our wealthy patron Dabney Horton.

    We picked up our own temporary police credentials and a file which had already been prepared for us. Both state and local police had been working hard, but there was absolutely no lead on the murderer.

    The three young women who had been killed were entirely unrelated and had different circles of friends. Everyone they knew had been questioned, every step they were known to have taken was traced and retraced, and still there was nothing to point to the killer. No suspicious characters, no suddenly appearing or disappearing boyfriends, nor any other strangers had surfaced in connection with any of the victims.

The three murdered women did have a few things in common. They were all very young: Two were nineteen, and one was twenty. They all lived in city neighborhoods in Richmond, and two of them did not own cars. All of them were thin, pretty and not very tall. They were all quiet and shy and perhaps somewhat lonely. The first and third victims were black, the second was white. The second and third victims were college students, the first was a young working woman.

Intervals of three weeks and then five weeks separated the three killings. All the women were raped, and all were slashed to death with an assortment of large knives, and all had been slashed and stabbed even after they were dead. The women had been bound and manacled in various ways while they had been tormented. Each body had been found a matter of some days – as long as two weeks – after death.

Every corpse had been dropped by the side of one of several long, twisty, sparsely-travelled and sparsely-populated country roads in rural Louisa, about forty miles north and west of Richmond. Louisa county is a quiet, slow, old-fashioned part of the state, with many people of modest incomes living a simple life that has not changed much in the last half a century.

The area where the bodies were found is an area of the county mostly populated, as Dabney Horton had indicated, by black families who had been on the same land since the end of slavery and Reconstruction. There was very little crime, ever, in that stable area of Louisa. Local residents were appalled and horrified that such awful murders had touched upon their doorstep. These country people rarely made any trip as far as Richmond city. Most of the locals had been interviewed, but there was no lead of any kind, not even a hint of a connection to a murderer in Richmond.

Three murders and no leads. Three young women raped and stabbed to death, perhaps kept alive for hours or days by their tormentor before dying in one last scream. The police were working around the clock, thinking, interviewing, looking; but they were not producing.

It was very clear to everyone, however, that if the killer wasn't caught, he would indeed be killing again.

* * *

Our second stop was with the city of Richmond detectives, who had very little to add to the information we received from the state police.

Amanda and I then got on the interstate to drive to Louisa county so we could meet with the police chief there where the bodies had been found. Our meeting with him was at the county morgue.

I'm not fond of dead bodies, and to me it seemed a grim duty to approach the morgue building and walk among the recently deceased.

As we approached the entrance I looked at Amanda and saw a peculiar glow on her face. She seemed intent, almost eager for the experience. Her pretty dark eyes had a faraway look, as if she could see something in the distance, something that was not apparent to me at all.

I stopped her stroll toward the building, and Amanda and I stood together for a moment in the little park near the morgue, the Virginia spring sunshine falling beautifully upon us.

"Amanda," I asked, "What are these special powers that you seem to have, that Dabney Horton talked about? What is it that you think we can do to find the murderer in this case, that the police with all their computers and experience can't? Why is it that you were kind enough to invite me in on this – not that I'm complaining – given that I don't have a clue as to what we're going to do or how to go about tracking an unknown murderer? Even if *you* have got special powers, I don't think *I* have any."

Amanda smiled, and looked at me with an expression that was warm and deep. I felt myself being seduced by her.

"Amanda," I said, "There *is* something unusual about you, isn't there? Tell me."

"Yes, I'll tell you," said Amanda. She paused. "Sometimes – but only sometimes – I can hear the voices of the dead."

It was a quiet moment there outside the Louisa morgue. The sun was shining, a gentle breeze was blowing, a few cars were passing in the street. I looked into the rich dark eyes of my detective friend Amanda Poe, and I realized that the strange thing she had just said was something she truly meant.

When she said, "I can hear the voices of the dead," I sensed a chill within me. I felt that she was telling the truth, and that through Amanda I really was connecting to a world beyond this one. Perhaps, I thought, she was *more* than merely human. Perhaps Amanda lived in feminine flesh in our world of light, and also in her spirit touched the world of darkness beyond the grave. In her beautiful brown eyes I knew there was mystery, there was truth, there was life, and there was death.

And still, I wanted to kiss her.

"How do you hear the dead?" I asked, in a sincere tone that surprised even myself. We sat down together on a white cast iron bench in the park.

"In odd ways, mostly," she replied. "Dreams, intuitions, feelings. Sometimes a word or phrase comes into my mind, and I know it's not from me or from anyone else living. But sometimes I even see faces, and feel the presence of the dead as much as I feel you're in front of me now. I've had these feelings ever since I was a little girl. They scared me then, and sometimes they even still scare me. But, in another way, I'm comfortable with the dead. They are as much a part of reality as anyone."

I sat quietly for a moment, pondering, trying to understand. "So," I began to ask, "In that case Horton was talking about, where you helped the family find the missing document, it was the dead who assisted you?"

Amanda laughed. "Yes, it was their dead ancestors who told me where it was buried.

Actually, they thought it was funny that all these people were so much in a tizzy about a casually buried document from the last century."

"*Who* thought it was funny?" I asked.

Amanda looked at me.

"You mean," I said, "It was the dead ancestors who thought it was funny?"

Amanda smiled, and then we both began to laugh.

"Well!" I exclaimed. "I'm glad that ghosts have a sense of humor!" I looked at the sidewalk and laughed a little nervously, not sure if I had just learned some new truths about the universe or whether I was beginning to lose my mind.

"So now," I said, "It's because of your ability to communicate with the world of the dead that we've got a chance at cracking this case, is that it? The dead might be able to point the way to the killers among the living?"

Amanda nodded. It was that simple to her. I shook my head at the astonishing strangeness of it all.

"You know, Amanda," I said, "I've spent my life learning to confront human dangers. I know how to protect myself against a human slimeball, how to draw my gun and shoot. But now that we're dealing with the dead, I wonder: Are we going to wind up in a situation we can't control, stirring up forces from the world beyond the grave?"

"You know, that's a question I've considered all my life," she answered. "I think that, in general, we don't need to be afraid of the dead. They're all around us, anyway, nearly all the time. It's true that a person can get involved with frightening forces he can't control. People have problems when they relate to the dead in ways that aren't right."

I was mentally lost. This was all a bit much. I looked up into the sky toward the sun – the symbol of life – and closed my eyes. I wondered if the ghosts of the dead were listening to our conversation. A feeling pierced me; and my eyes shot open and I almost jumped. Damn, I felt that the dead *were* listening!

Amanda touched my arm gently. "David, don't worry. The things to fear from the dead, are the same things to fear from the living. If there is evil within you, the evil dead will connect to that evil and build on it. For those people who are good in their hearts, the dead can comfort and even protect us, in a shadowy sort of way.

"But," she continued, "It is true that talking to the dead changes us, it brings us into places that might be a little scary. That's even part of why I need you, David. I need you to be with me on the dark journey ahead, just like I was with you on that street when you fired your gun."

I loved the sound of Amanda's voice, and I had loved hearing her say, "I need you, David." Her words seemed seductive and almost romantic. I could not consider refusing her request that I accompany her on this strange journey, even if it meant visiting with ghosts and devils and terrors beyond the grave. I resolved to be Amanda's loyal friend, regardless of what strange things lay in store for us.

"Amanda," I said, "How can I help you when I can't see or hear what you can see and hear?"

"Oh, David, there's much *more* to you than you know," she answered. "You're a very comforting person. You're a companion not only to walk with on a tough city street, but also for here, right now, as we're about to go into a morgue and maybe tomorrow visit a cemetery. You have a very solid inner being, you're the kind of person the dead respect.

"And what's more, David," she added, "I know you're not afraid of the dead. That's why you can shoot so fast."

I looked at her with puzzlement.

"Most people," Amanda explained, "Most people couldn't be gunfighters because of that split second of hesitation, when the other person is raising his gun and you have to shoot immediately if you want to live at all.

"Part of the fear of killing another human being is your subconscious knowledge that killing that person will put you into immediate contact with the dead person's ghost. As you kill someone, the dead person's spirit rises up in front of you and looks at you. And some secret part of you looks back at that ghost, and you confront the fact this other person *is* a ghost because of you.

"Most people are afraid to see this ghost, even if it means losing one's own life in the process. But a true gunfighter is a person who will shoot without hesitation, who is ready and unafraid to face the ghosts of the people he kills.

"When you shot those two bad guys who were trying to molest that girl on Franklin Street, you didn't hesitate an instant. You shot your pistol quickly, accurately and immediately. They were evil men, and they became horrible-looking ghosts. I rarely *see* the dead, but as you killed them, I saw their spirits, ugly, monstrous spirits rising up from their bodies. They looked at you, and they looked at me, and they looked at the girl whom they'd tried to kidnap – that's when she screamed. But you didn't flinch. Somewhere beneath your conscious experience, you saw them, too: The ghosts of the men you killed. You saw them, you came to know them, but you didn't care. You had done the right thing. What you cared about was the safety of that young woman, and the safety of the other people on the street. You looked death right in the eye, and it didn't deflect or delay your actions one instant.

"Yes, David, you are a special man. This murder case we're on now is going to be difficult, and I know we're going to run into some frightening things. But I knew when Dabney called me, that you were exactly the right person to work with me, whether we face dangers from the living or from the dead."

I felt humbled by her trust in me, and confused by the supernatural world Amanda was revealing. "I hope I never let you down," I said. And with that we got up and went into the morgue.

* * *

It was cold in the morgue and it smelled bad. The county medical examiner was waiting for us.

On a slab there was presented the body of Tayisha Jones, the murderer's third victim. She had been a young, attractive, gentle-faced woman with short, waved hair. There were slash marks on her face, and another cut on her neck that extended below the sheet which lay across her shoulders.

For a moment we were all silent. Amanda Poe looked intent and even a bit angelic as she stood by the forepart of the slab. She touched the victim's forehead. "Peace," she said, seemingly forgetting there were others in the room. Amanda seemed to glow with an expression that suggested to me the concept of friendship.

The sheet was withdrawn from the victim's body. Horrible, deep knife-slashes covered the young woman's corpse. Large bruises covered her wrists and ankles as if she had been bound for a long period. "Very similar to the first two killings," noted the medical examiner. "In every case we didn't have the body until a week or more after the victim died. It seems that the perpetrator held her, played with her, and tortured her for a substantial amount of time while she lived. She was bound with metal shackles that were very old – there were traces of rust on both her wrists and her ankles.

"It seems, too, that the killer held her for at least a day or two after death, that the corpse was further mutilated and used even after the girl was dead. What's very unusual, too, is the attention devoted to clean-up. After this person's pleasure was finished, the corpse was thoroughly washed and wiped with antiseptic solutions, and even the hair was shampooed. The body that was left in a garbage bag on the road was quite uniquely prepared by the murderer."

I brought the sheet back up to cover the body's shoulders. I could look no more. Amanda's eyes were already focused far away. The Louisa police chief came in. He had little to offer.

"We've talked to everybody," he assured us. "I think there's only one killer, with this kind of detailed personal perversion showing in the abuse of each victim. There's the racial element with the first and third victims being black, and the bodies dropped in a black neighborhood of the county, but for the life of me we can't figure out what else there is to it. We're watching the roads to see if anyone suspicious appears, but there's a lot of miles of highways and we're just a small police force. Even with the troopers helping, someone could sneak in and out with

53

another body and we might still miss it. Who knows, maybe there's even another body out there!

"We've got word from Richmond you're some kind of special agents. We're glad to work with anyone who might be of help. If there's anything you need, let me know."

* * *

Seeing the actual body of a murder victim immediately personalizes the whole case for you. Now, murder had a face, and our task of finding the killer had now become a personal one. In the lobby of the morgue I thought about that murdered girl and what kind of life she might have had, what kind of future for her that would never be fulfilled.

I thought about the killer, chaining up his victim, raping her, torturing her, cutting and slashing her until she died. How many hours of horror did that poor girl undergo before she perished? It was hard to see any penalty adequate to punish such a crime.

Amanda and I walked out again back into the Virginia sun, away from the cold and smell of the morgue and back into the land of the living. When the police chief and medical examiner were out of sight, I asked Amanda: "Well, did you feel or hear anything from the dead girl's spirit? Was she able to help us?"

It seemed like I was already taking for granted that Amanda could communicate with the dead. The strangeness of my question didn't hit me until after I had spoken it.

"I felt *something*," said Amanda. "But I couldn't hear." She looked concerned. "I felt that she was a good woman, and that she was now at peace. She seemed glad we were trying to help, and she wanted to tell us something. But there was another voice interfering: someone shouting, someone screaming something awful. And the result was, I could hear nothing at all."

"Was it her own screaming?" I asked. "Was it the echoes of her own agony under torture before she died?"

"No, it was not her," said Amanda, with confidence.

"It was the killer, then, wasn't it? The murderer maybe was sending out some kind of psychic wave to block your communication."

"No," said Amanda, "Definitely not. The murderer is a living being. The screaming I was hearing was another voice from the dead."

I felt very cold all of a sudden. "Any idea who?"

"I have no face, no name, no identity, just screaming and evil. But whoever that ghost is, I think that ghost is who we have to find first."

"So what you're saying," I said, trying to follow her mind, "Is that before we go looking for the killer we've got to find a ghost."

"And we've got to make him shut up," said Amanda, nodding.

"That sounds difficult," I said. "Maybe a little frightening."

"That's why I need you," she said, smiling a little. "The two of us together can probably do it."

I tried to smile a little, too. It was all very strange, but I was beginning to understand. And I was eager to assist Amanda and do the job,

even if it meant trespassing into the world
beyond this one.

The Pastor's Secret

The next morbid task for Amanda and me was to visit the graves of the other two murder victims. From the Louisa morgue we drove about thirty-five miles northwest to a cemetery in Culpeper, a small, old town in the heart of Virginia.

It was mid-afternoon when we entered through the cemetery gates with their plaques memorializing Confederate soldiers who had died in the Civil War. The sky was sunny but the air had begun to cool.

As far as we could see, on this weekday we were alone in the large necropolis. Small and medium-sized tombstones were arranged in neat rows up and down the gentle cemetery hills, while larger stones and mausoleums formed a

59

brooding skyline in the distance. Amanda was wearing a lacy black shawl, and she walked among the graves with an erect, proud posture and a careful, deliberate step that I had not noticed before. She seemed lost in thought, her face once again aglow just as she had appeared in the morgue.

For me, a cemetery had always seemed a dreary and drab place, a waste of good land that marred nature with symbols of death and decay. But as I walked by Amanda Poe's side, I felt *connected* to the buried dead somehow. It was an eerie but beautiful sensation.

The sky above was sunny and nearly cloudless, but I could *feel* a darkness, as if a shroud of death encircled this sunny world and was about to close in around it. For a moment I felt a storm coming, dark clouds looming in around me, even though my eyes saw only sunshine and light. The clouds encircled me, there were faces in the sky, voices seemed about to talk – My heart thumped in terror.

I looked at Amanda and she smiled, a wise, very knowing smile. She *knew* what I had seen. She had seen the same thing, although for her it was obviously familiar. I began to understand Amanda better. I did not say a word.

"This way," said Amanda. We soon arrived at the grave of Cynthia Roseman, the second of the murder victims.

Amanda dropped to her knees and sat, like one might sit with a friend at a picnic. I stood respectfully. Amanda gently put her hand on the young woman's grave.

I closed my eyes. Images began to form. I saw a young, pretty girl, bound and gagged. Her eyes showed terror and pleaded for mercy. Then the face of the girl grew calm and looked at me. She wanted to speak, wanted to talk, but the gag was still in place.

I opened my eyes and saw Amanda still sitting by the young woman's grave. Amanda's face was calm and peaceful. For a long minute she sat and I stood, and we listened and heard nothing but the blowing of a soft wind.

"She's not getting through," said Amanda. "I feel it's the same entity blocking us, too, the same as at the morgue." She looked toward the headstone. "Rest peacefully, my young friend," she said, "We'll find the truth and free you." I felt a chill as a dark wave of emotion swept over me.

"We have an enemy," said Amanda.

"You mean," I said, "Not just the murderer, but a ghost who doesn't want us to hear the victim speak?"

Amanda nodded.

"Is this poor girl still suffering?" I asked.

"Only in a small way," said Amanda. "She is in a place where she cannot be harmed any longer in the way she was violated while she lived. But she does want to tell us what happened, and she needs that truth to be known before she is totally at peace."

As we left the cemetery I could still feel the voices and faces around us, only they no longer made me so afraid as before. Maybe, I thought, it was all my imagination. But maybe, now that I was spending time with Amanda in places like this, I too was getting used to sensing the presence of the dead.

* * *

At twilight of that day Amanda and I were still together, back in Richmond. We were in another cemetery, the famous Hollywood cemetery in the center of Richmond where Confederate President Jeff Davis and many other notables are buried.

We were not alone there. Small groups of students and tourists strolled among the crowded gravesites. Some of the students shared liquor or marijuana, making a gauche and decadent display amid the tombs.

We found the grave of the first of the victims. Her name was Cassandra Williams, and due to her sad urban murder she had been honored with a place in this most famous of all Richmond cemeteries. The stone was small but of a beautiful colored marble. I felt a certain closeness to the victim there at her grave, but I did not have the same feelings or images come to mind as I had experienced this afternoon at the cemetery in Culpeper.

Maybe it was because of the students drinking and smoking, or maybe because of the fact that I had toured Hollywood cemetery so many times before with friends who were visiting town; in any case, this visit remained all too ordinary for me, and I did not have any supernatural sensations.

For Amanda, however, it was another story. I kept a watchful eye for our surroundings while she herself sat, once again, alongside a murder victim's grave. For a time she seemed lost in thought, listening for a voice from beyond. Then she opened her eyes and spoke.

"It's the same."

I nodded. "So someone's not letting these poor souls talk to us?"

"That's right," said Amanda. "But I think I know now where to start looking."

As we departed the famous cemetery gate I asked: "Where to next, my dear guide to the netherworld?"

Amanda looked at me crossly. I guess I had been making fun of her.

"If you're not nice," she said, "I'm not going to tell you."

I know that one of the worst offenses a man can commit is not to take a woman seriously. I did my best to look sheepish and embarrassed. "Sorry," I mumbled.

After a moment Amanda continued: "The key, I think, is exactly what's most puzzling to the police – where the bodies were dropped. Why did this killer drive forty miles to dump these bodies on a country road, when the James River is right here with a thousand places to drop something quietly in the river?

"When I was here by Cassandra's grave, I felt the same silence, the same repression, the same urge to speak that I felt with the other victims. But I also saw the road, the road in Louisa where her body was dropped. And I've never been there in my life.

"That's the key, David. Somewhere alongside those roads in Louisa county. We won't find the killer there, but we will find that ghost who's getting in our way. We need to have a talk with him."

She sounded so matter-of-fact about it. Oh sure, find a local ghost and go talk to him. Ring his doorbell and ask him questions while he flies to and fro before us.

I thought about the gun beneath my jacket. A gun stoked with deep-penetrating bullets that would waste virtually any human adversary. But what about confronting a ghost? Especially a malicious ghost who was trying to silence murder victims and who might be in league with a killer! That gun in my holster might not be of much use in opposing a demon from beyond the grave.

"Tomorrow to Louisa county?" I asked, hoping that Amanda was not intending to go there now. I'd spent enough time among the dead for one day. Amanda agreed.

We stopped briefly at a coffee shop, and then I drove her home. I watched Amanda's lace-adorned figure disappear safely behind her front door.

I drove on to my house, reflecting upon how I had matured beyond my previous limitations. A couple of weeks before, I had faced two bad guys and shot them dead. Now the dead were my daily companions, and I was getting used to thinking of them right alongside the living.

In the course of a few days I had come to accept the existence of ghosts and voices from the dead as real and true. Just being with

Amanda, I had already accepted some of her way of looking at the world.

I thought about Amanda, with her seemingly supernatural powers of feeling and communicating beyond this world. What it must have been like for her, to grow up knowing she could hear the voices of the dead! What moments of terror and wonder there must have been in her childhood!

It was all strange, quite eerie indeed. At the same time, I felt a strong pull of attraction to Amanda, an attraction that was both sexual and much, much deeper. Making love to her, I felt, would be a very profound experience, an act of intimacy that would extend into the realms of the spirit.

Amanda Poe was clearly a woman of an extraordinary nature. With her sensitivities, I knew she could never be lied to or deceived. If anything were to develop between Amanda and myself, my heart would have to be in the right place, absolutely pure. I wouldn't want Amanda's ghostly friends come to haunt me!

This last notion made me laugh out loud as I was parking my car. I imagined Amanda, one dark night after an argument with me, calling ghosts into her living room: "Yes, you ghosts," she would say, "Go and get that wicked David Allan!" And for an offense of wronging Amanda Poe, my penalty might be that of being haunted into madness!

As I exited my car I checked the street carefully, as always, before locking the vehicle and going up the walk to my townhouse. Once inside I sat down to think.

I knew that, before I could even begin to understand the subject of ghosts, or hope to develop my relationship with Amanda, my primary focus in life needed to be our mission of finding the creep who was this savage murderer of young women.

Whatever the supernatural detours of our investigation, the fact was that we needed to find an all-too-human killer who shackled women, raped them, and used large knives to cut them up while they were still living, and who then with further bloody jabs imposed a screaming, terrible and too-early death.

For the goal of catching this murderer, it would be worth going to hell and back. I was beginning to appreciate that Amanda had chosen me as her companion because she knew I was a good man to make the journey with her.

I went to sleep that night with care and deliberateness, a loaded pistol near my hand and a prayer upon my lips.

* * *

The next day was a turning point, not only in the investigation, but also in my life.

Amanda and I had breakfast at a Church Hill restaurant and then drove out to Louisa county, to travel its byways and find our ghost. Somewhere out there was an evil presence, a presence from beyond the grave who *knew* about these murders. Our journey to the countryside felt quite gloomy despite the sunshine overhead.

As we drove out to find the wooded roads where the bodies of the murder victims had been found, a lot of strange feelings stirred within me. I was afraid, I was curious, I was anxious. I knew I would be confronting terrors of a type I had never seen before. But we had to go. This was our job, to face the dead to save the living.

I looked over at Amanda sitting in the front car seat next to me. As usual she was dressed in dark colors. She was barely more than a hundred pounds of intelligent, beautiful, gun-toting womanhood.

I thought about her body, and even imagined what it looked like underneath those clothes. The fantasy of seeing Amanda unclothed gave me great pleasure, and even a bit of courage. I said to myself that, if this vulnerable, slight young woman is brave enough to face the dead and go find a killer, it was not for me to hesitate or be afraid. I mentally reaffirmed my resolve to be at her side till our job was done. I would face whatever terrors she would face, whether they be from this world or from the world beyond the grave.

Amanda turned and smiled at me. Her smile was to me like a kiss, given by a medieval lady to a knight in shining armor. Her kind acknowledgment of me was an inspiration that I would treasure. So I smiled, too.

* * *

With county map in hand, we visited the three places on back country roads where the bodies of the victims had been dropped. Our visits were solemn, as we imagined the killer's car pausing on these sparsely-toured byways to unload a garbage bag with the remains of a mutilated young woman.

The bodies had been discovered in one case by a hiker, in two other cases by locals who had been drawn to investigate the gathering of animals near the festering roadside corpses.

These wooded roads were peaceful, beautiful and green in the lovely Virginia springtime. Amanda and I gathered no specific clues from the sites where the bodies had been found. We felt it was helpful to be touring the neighborhood, but the path to follow was not immediately apparent.

As we drove up and down the Louisa backroads – narrow pathways of asphalt without lines or markings, the edges overgrown with brush and trees – we felt transported back in time whenever we passed a row of homes. The dwellings were somewhat less than houses, often just mere shacks, usually with a tumble-down porch and a crooked chimney. Most were very small, and many were obviously built fifty or eighty or even a hundred years ago. Some did not have plumbing, and there were outhouses to be seen behind them.

In this country neighborhood, the resident families were mostly black and poor. Most of the cars in driveways were old, bent and rusted, and some of them were clearly not running at all.

Still, there was a gracious feeling to the area despite the lack of material means. Poor conditions in a country area is quite different from poverty in the city. There was no sign of tension or crime or fear. Children played happily in large country yards, and adults of various ages sat on their porches or worked on their crops and gardens at an unhurried pace. People would wave to us as we drove slowly past, and Amanda and I would wave back.

It all felt so friendly and warm, so safe and good, even if it was clear that few people had money enough to qualify as middle class.

My own late model car identified me as wealthy by comparison, but I still felt welcome among these good poor country folk. It was an unlikely place for a psychopathic killer to want to leave his corpses.

As we drove, I hit on the idea of going to talk with the neighborhood preacher. A country preacher is as knowledgeable as anyone about what really goes on in the area he serves. So Amanda and I drove back to a small but obviously thriving church we had noticed less than a mile from one of the places where a murder victim had been found.

Elijah Baptist Church was a classic early 1800s church building in nearly perfect condition. Unlike the run-down homes in the area, the church was well-kept and beautiful: Fresh white siding and coated aluminum trim, windows perfectly painted and caulked, a shiny church bell atop the steeple. Adjacent to the church was a medium-size frame house, also well-maintained. This was the parsonage where the minister lived. There was manicured green grass everywhere, and a black Cadillac in the pastor's driveway. The sign on the church said he was the Rev. James I. Willis.

Amanda and I knocked on the door. A friendly face answered. "Good afternoon!" he said, in a rich and deep voice. "I'm Pastor Willis. How can I help you folks? Would you like to come in?"

We went inside and were offered iced lemonade, sweetened to perfection. The friendly pastor made small talk and didn't even press us as to why we were there. It was good old country friendliness, the kind where there is always time for an easy chat before getting down to business. The pastor's wife was away shopping and his children were at school, so we were free to discuss our grim concern about the slashed bodies found in the neighborhood.

"We've prayed every Sunday that the killer might be found," said the pastor. "And we've prayed for the killer, that he might come to confess his sins and repent before God.

"In the eight years that I've been pastor," he continued, "I don't know of anything that has upset this community as much as these murders and those bodies being left here. The good people of this area somehow feel they are part of this, even though I'm absolutely sure no one local is to blame.

"By the way," he added, "Do you know of Dabney Horton? He's someone who might be able to help."

Amanda and I were both surprised. We had told the pastor we were investigators working on the murders, but we had omitted the fact that we had been hired by the wealthy Horton. I wondered, Why was his name popping up now?

"Everyone knows of Dabney Horton," said Amanda. "I've met his wife a number of times, and both of us know Dabney. In fact, he hired us. How do you know him?"

"I'll tell you folks a secret if you promise you won't spread it around the neighborhood," said the pastor. We nodded. "You know who pays for this church? Dabney Horton. He's the secret source of our budget. He arranged for the renovations, he gives most of our annual budget, he pays for my living expenses.

"That Cadillac you see out there was bought and paid for by Dabney Horton. After

I'd been pastor about six months, I got a call from Mr. Horton and he asked me to meet him in Richmond on Broad Street. We met at a restaurant across the way from the Cadillac dealership, and he gave me a car.

"I tried to say no. I thought it was too flashy for a poor neighborhood like this. But old Dabney thought the people here would like to see their pastor in a nice car, something that they could ride in every once in a while, too. You know, he was right. The Cadillac you see outside is the second one he's bought for me. He made me trade the first one for a newer model!

"Dabney Horton gives me money that I use in the community. If a child needs a medical bill paid, if some family really needs something, the money comes from Dabney. The people don't know this, they think it's just the general church fund. A few of the old-timers, though, they've figured it out, they know that Dabney is really our patron.

"You see, the Horton family really owns all this land out here, or did own it. A few folks here own their own homesteads, but in many cases people here still have their land on squatter's rights."

"Squatter's rights?" asked Amanda.

"Yes," said pastor Willis. "In the time of the Civil War the Horton plantation here had hundreds of slaves. Many people here are descendants of those slaves. When the white masters went off to die in the Civil War, the Hortons – who were really among the best and most gentle of the slave owners – gave their servants 'squatter's rights' on this land. This means these people and their children, and their children's children, and all their descendants, can stay on this land forever. They can't sell it, they can't borrow against it, but it's theirs to live on.

"They could give it up and walk away from it, or not pay the property taxes on it, in which case it goes back to the Horton family. But Dabney Horton is not trying to take his land back. In fact, he's paid the taxes for people in trouble so they can continue staying on it. He's a great man, he's kept this whole community alive with his money. When I pray, he's the first person I pray for."

"So all this area," I said, "All this is still on the books as Horton family land, except that the residents have squatter's rights for as many generations as they stay."

"That's right," said the pastor, "For miles around it's all the old Horton plantation. I hope you can help solve these murders, because it's something that can ultimately destroy this community. People are already talking about leaving their old homesteads and moving to the city.

"For some of the younger people, I understand. I encourage them to go to school and get a good job wherever they can find it. But for many folks here, they've got few skills, they can barely read or write their name, there would be no good life for them in Richmond. It's better for their souls to stay here."

We asked the pastor if there was anything he could tell us that might be helpful.

"Nothing comes to mind," he said. "I've kept my ears open, and I have no clue, no guesses, no idea of what might lead to finding this killer. I have no idea what possessed him to leave those bodies among my parishioners. But

I should say, too, that though I've been here eight years now, I'm just getting to know the area.

"But if I were you," he added, "I might talk with one or two of the older folks. You might start with Rachel Walker, she's over eighty, but she's a wise woman, and she was born in the same house she lives in now. If there's something in this neighborhood or its past that could help you, she's the one to ask. She has no phone but I'll tell you how to get to her place. She always enjoys visitors."

We stayed on at the parsonage a little longer, and then we bade farewell. It was interesting to learn that Dabney Horton was historically the real owner of this neighborhood where the murder victims' bodies had been abandoned. It was also interesting that Horton *didn't* tell us this when he hired us to pursue the investigation.

Amanda and I both felt there was yet more to be learned about the connection between these murders and the millionaire Hortons. Why did Dabney Horton want us to provide *him* with information before telling the police? We wondered out loud: Would the trail of the murderer lead us back to the door of the man who had hired us?

Mansion in the Weeds

That afternoon, we found ourselves in front of the old cottage inhabited by Rachel Walker, 84-year-old grand dame of the Louisa county neighborhood that had now become a sad depository for murder victims. Ms. Walker was youthful and sprightly; I would have guessed her age at about twenty years younger.

Her home was a fine, small house built about 1890 using the kind of large oaken beams rarely seen in construction today. The ceiling was low and the windows were off-center. Despite her long life there the furnishings were simple, although some pretty quilts and pillows adorned the living room and gave her home a comfortable character.

Rachel and Amanda hit it off immediately. After some gracious samplings of a pitcher of iced tea, the old woman turned to Amanda and said: "You've got the sight, haven't you? You see things, you hear things. You're young but you're wise. You've already touched the world beyond, the world that I will see in a few years after I leave this house forever."

Amanda smiled. Rachel touched her, and then looked at me. "You're a very lucky young man," she said. "You should stay close by Amanda, and trust her with everything. There are many adventures ahead for the two of you!"

Rachel told us stories about Louisa county history and about her own grandmother, who had been born a slave. It was a very pleasant afternoon, with no sound to disturb us other than the birds and crickets in the garden, and the ticking of an old clock. Sitting there with Rachel, we were touching the old Virginia that is now mostly just a faded memory.

Finally our talk turned to our investigation and the bodies on the road. Rachel surprised us with her quick confidence that she could point us in the right direction.

"Yes," said Rachel, "There is an old evil here that has come back, that is not yet sleeping. I think you can start to find what you need at the Old Mansion in the woods. If you do not discover your road to the truth after visiting there, I will be a very surprised old woman."

"The Old Mansion?" I asked. Amanda and I were both puzzled. But inside of me I felt my heart beat faster as it clouded with fear and foreboding. I already shared Rachel Walker's intuition that, whatever this Old Mansion was, it was a place on the road to confronting the murderer.

"The Old Mansion," Rachel repeated. Her eyes grew misty and distant. "Seventy years ago," she said, "Seventy years ago!"

"What happened, darling?" asked Amanda. "What happened to you, so long in the past?"

"I'll tell you what happened seventy years ago," said Rachel. She laughed. "It was the biggest whippin' I ever got! A girlfriend and I were thirteen. We had gone off wandering and found it, an old plantation house from before the war, the war that freed us from slavery.

Maggie and I – she was my girlfriend – we even went inside. We'd been told about the old house, and been warned never to go near it, but we were bad girls and went and explored it.

"It scared us, it seemed haunted. But nothing happened while we were there, except the wind made noise and the old house creaked and moaned while we walked through it. It wasn't long before Maggie and I ran away from it and went back home.

"That evening I wanted to brag, so at dinner I told the family that I had gone to see the Old Mansion and it wasn't anything special. I said it was just an old big house, that's all.

"As I talked at the table my mother's lips began to tremble. My father stared at the floor. They took me by the hand and led me away from the dinner table. Usually they'd wait till after dinner and punish us after the dishes were done, but this didn't wait a minute.

"We went to my mother's bedroom and she made me take off every stitch of clothing till I was plumb naked. Then she began to switch me, switch me hard. Then my father came in, and he took the switch and he began to whip me, even harder. I screamed and I cried and I bled from the whippin'. Oh, Lordy, it was terrible! They made me promise, promise in the name of Jesus, that I would never ever go back to the Old Mansion again, and that I would teach my own children never to go there, and that I would give them the same whippin' if they ever even *thought* about going there.

"For two more nights I got more whippin's, and I had to make the same promises. I never forgot my promises and I never went back to the big old house. My folks went to Maggie's folks – that's the girl that had gone with me – and she got some whippin's, too. When I raised my own young 'uns I gave 'em each a talk and a whippin' and I told 'em the devil would take 'em if they ever went there, and I don't think they ever disobeyed me.

"I tell you what, I think the devil is at that old house. I never learned the secret of why the Old Mansion is left alone, and why they let the weeds grow up around it.

"When these poor girls were killed just this last month or two, and their bodies were lyin' on the roads, I knew right away it's got somethin' to do with the Old Mansion. Maybe the whippin's I got saved me from ending up like those dead girls.

"But if you two have got courage, and you've got the Lord with you, I feel in my heart that the Old Mansion is where you've got to go and start lookin' for who did this. But both of you, both of you!" – she almost shouted this – "Both of you keep an eye open for Satan! You might look in his face while you're there, and don't you let him take you."

Amanda nodded earnestly. I could tell from Amanda's expression that she believed Rachel was right as to where we needed to go next. Amanda took Rachel's elderly hand and touched it to her own cheek. "I'm sorry you got such a bad whipping," said Amanda.

"Well, a whippin's not the worst thing," said Rachel. "Maybe it did me some good, Lord knows!"

We stayed on a while longer visiting, and we learned exactly how to find the Old Mansion, given that the old roads were now unmarked and overgrown. There was a place we could park our car off the road, at a spot used by picnickers and deer hunters. From there it was about a mile through thick brush, then across a shallow stream to the plantation grounds, and finally about another three quarters of a mile to the old house, the old house where we hoped to find a clue to help catch a serial murderer.

We thanked Rachel Walker for her time, and we went on our way as the dinner hour approached. Amanda and I proceeded into town for a quiet meal at a diner near the Louisa courthouse.

At the diner we asked about the old abandoned plantation house. The waitress' husband, who was also the chef, came out to talk to us. Yes, he said, it was there, but few locals had ever seen it. There were all sorts of stories about it, tales of people who had gone to take a look at it and never returned, of hunters from the city who followed a deer trail onto the grounds and never lived to tell what they saw.

Yes, people hunted in the woods not too far away from it, but our host warned us never to cross the stream that formed the border of the Old Mansion grounds. That was the realm of the devil, according to common view, and by local custom it was simply avoided, generation after generation.

Our dinner was somber as we thought of the task ahead of us. Before nightfall we would see the Old Mansion and maybe meet a ghost or, who knew, perhaps even the devil. And maybe, just maybe, we would be a little closer to drawing a bead on a killer of young women.

* * *

It was still three hours before dark when Amanda and I parked my car in the little clearing by the picnic tables, about to begin our foot-journey toward the Old Mansion. We had both worn good outdoor boots for our day out in the country, and in my car's trunk I had a small camping kit, including a large sleeping bag. "Let's take it," said Amanda, "We might want to spend the night at the old house." I looked at her and realized she was serious. This ghost-hunting stuff was for real.

The thought of spending a night in some spooky old abandoned building gave me the chills, though I didn't argue with Amanda. I felt, though, that I would rather be back on the Richmond streets facing a gang of drug dealers, than be trooping through these ancient woods looking for ghosts. But here I was with Amanda, and this seemed to be what we needed to do to catch a murderous psychopath. So I silently assembled our gear, and we set off out into the woods.

The first mile, toward the stream, was not hard. Hunters had used trails here for many a year, and while the undergrowth was thick it was not hard to penetrate. It was not deer season, and indeed we spotted a family of deer in the distance. This was central Virginia somewhat as it must have looked to its earliest settlers.

Then, Amanda and I came to the shallow stream which marked the boundary between the regular woods frequented by hunters and hikers, and the no-man's-land that surrounded the old plantation house. It was the point of decision, the edge of no return.

Across the water we saw tall trees and thick brush. In the air above the water there was a thick mist with a strange, sickly smell. Upstream a little on the other side, there was a male deer with an unusually dark brown color and short antlers. This stag looked at us with a penetrating gaze.

It all seemed strange. We waded across the stream, careful to keep our gear and guns dry. We set foot on the other side, and the ground felt squishy. We sank a little in the mud. I felt unsafe, and I looked protectively toward Amanda.

"This is the way," she said. She was sure we were on the road to finding the killer, in one way or another. I knew it was my job to go along. We headed into the undergrowth.

In addition to the semi-automatic pistol in my shoulder holster, I had a .41 magnum revolver on my hip. The chambers were loaded alternately with hand-loaded snakeshot and with heavyweight hollowpoints. In the wild, a large-caliber revolver is the preferred hiker's weapon.

In the distance we heard something which seemed to be a bear growling. It was unlikely to find a bear in this part of the state, but I wondered if, because of the way the land around the old plantation house had been avoided over the years, maybe a group of bears had somehow made a home base here unnoticed by modern development.

In our left hands Amanda and I wielded large brush knives to hack our way through some of the thicker undergrowth. Even with the growth, though, it was clear we were following some sort of trail. I wondered how much the area had changed in the seventy years since Rachel Walker made her one and only journey through these woods. Were we taking the same trail Rachel had taken?

Ahead of me the grass moved. It was a snake. I drew my gun quickly and fired one perfectly aimed blast. The snake died instantly from the densely spread no. 12 shot in my gun. The snake was not of the poisonous type, it turned out, and so my killing was regretful. But I had thought it was better to be safe than to deal with the problems of poisonous snakebite.

The gun blast made me think of how easy it would be to die in these woods and have no one ever know, given how rarely these woods were entered by human feet. Some killer could easily pick off Amanda and me with a simple scoped deer rifle. The thought made me wish we had told the local sheriff where we were going. Not that this would save us, but at least someone would come afterwards to find our bodies.

Thoughts of death and murder and killing filled my brain as we proceeded. Amanda and I were silent. She moved forward very intently. For her, this was obviously a journey of discovery. For me, it was an unpleasant foray into unworldly ambiguity. I longed to see again the spacious interior of my automobile parked back at the clearing. How nice it would be to sit in those plush seats again and turn the key and drive away down the road back into civilization!

It seemed we walked a long time. For a while the path seemed endless. And then, suddenly, the terminus was clear. Ahead was a clearing. Strange, large flowers loomed up in this space between the trees. We had stumbled upon a part of the old estate.

The clearing was an old cemetery, and beneath the tall grass and strange plants and flowers were tombstones more than a century old. The names and dates were mostly faded. I looked up at Amanda, and she seemed intoxicated, energized, almost crazed. She began to move and whirl, and almost dance amid the graves. She moved quickly from one stone to another, like a debutante at a party, as if she was flirting, gossiping, teasing. Around and around the clearing she moved, a half-smile upon her lips, her cape twirling about her shoulders.

I looked down at the ground and saw my boot was next a small stone. I moved my foot and saw the last name. "Horton," it said. I stepped back, and found I was treading upon another grave. I realized bodies were buried tightly one upon another. Amanda paused her unusual dance.

"A family in time," she said. "The house is just a little further. Let's go."

* * *

I thought Amanda was somewhat strange, but yet I still trusted her. In fact, I desired her. But I was not prepared for this project to which we were committed. This was a voyage meant for a different kind of traveller than myself.

We moved on. Shortly, up through the trees, we got a glimpse of a mass of white stone half-covered with moss. As we proceeded, other parts of the structure became visible.

We were there at last. The Old Mansion, an old plantation house, left alone for a century. Weeds and tall grasses grew right up to its foundation now, and its former lawns were dotted with hundred-year-old trees.

It had obviously been a fine building in its day. Made of white stone that was now moss-covered and chipped, it was not as large as other plantation houses but it was obviously substantial. There was a carriage entrance on the ground, a large porch above it with columns, and a flat roof. It was a narrow three-story building that would have six or so bedrooms inside.

On the top floor most of the glass was broken. The main floor, however, seemed to have much of the original glass intact, and the building as a whole seemed sound. It was actually remarkable that such a fine country house had been abandoned. There was definitely a story to be learned here. Given the

Southern love of tradition and fine old homes, it was quite unusual that this place would have been left to rot for a century and more.

"You know who still probably owns this place?" said Amanda, almost rhetorically.

"Our boss Dabney Horton," I said, and Amanda nodded.

"What a great place," she exclaimed.

"Not at the moment it isn't," I said.

We climbed the front steps over the carriage entrance and stood on the porch between the columns. "There were good times here once," said Amanda, with authority. "There were carriages coming up the long driveway that's hidden now by all the trees and grass. Ladies in long dresses sipped drinks on the porch, and gentlemen flirted with them chivalrously. It must have been quite a place.

"But," she continued, "There's something else here, too, something awful. You know, David, coming here was the right thing to do. The beginning of our answer is *right here.*"

We headed for the front door. My left hand reached for the doorknob, and then I was shocked to notice that I was holding my pistol in my right hand. Without even noticing it, I had such a sense of danger I had drawn my gun and popped off the safety. We were here in the woods by an abandoned house and I was ready to shoot, like a cop on a raid.

"Good idea," said Amanda, and she drew her own gun. The door-lock was not functional and the door opened easily.

Just to one side of the heavy mansion doors was a beautiful, empty, cobweb-filled drawing room. There was a magnificent marble fireplace, and the old plaster walls glowed in the early evening light that gently passed through the imperfect window glass. For a moment I had a fantasy that Amanda and I would settle down someday in a house like this. It appeared the floors and walls were still solid, and so we proceeded to inspect the building. There was no sign anyone had been there in any recent year. There were no furnishings or personal items anywhere in this main part of the house.

Upstairs there was broken glass and stains from water damage, but the roof was still holding and it was clear the house could still be fixed up and lived in.

We went outside and explored the downstairs through the carriage entrance. Here we did find some heavy nineteenth century junk: Pots, boxes, large chunks of broken furniture.

We also found a heavy oaken door that looked as if it connected to a root cellar. There was a heavy iron ring on the outside.

"There! He's in there!" shouted Amanda.

I pointed my pistol and looked intently at the door. "How do you know?" I said quietly.

"Maybe not the killer," she said. "But it's our ghost, our demon. That's *his* room."

"So if we go in?" I asked. Amanda was more of an expert about these things than me.

"We have to go in," she said, without answering my question.

With one hand I pulled at the door. It didn't give. "Cover me," I said, holstering my gun. Amanda held her own pistol and a flashlight, while I pulled at the door handle with full strength. It was definitely locked.

"I can pick it, I think," I said. Every good detective always carries his lock-picking kit, and I pulled mine out of my pack. A little lubricant in the lock, standard master skeleton key, and the rusty iron mechanism budged and then clicked. I pulled the door open sharply, and Amanda flashed a light inside while I drew my own gun.

Several rats on the dirt floor froze, hypnotized by the sudden brightness. We threw the light around the small room in a brief search for larger presences, and then we turned the light off so the rats could leave. Two of the rats decided to go out through the door we had opened, and they scurried over Amanda's boots and she shrieked. I opened the front door of the house and the rats were gone.

We turned both our flashlights on and then entered the musty chamber that had been so long sealed. It smelled awful. It was a room about twelve by fifteen, and there was a little bit of wood flooring, but the surface was mostly dirt.

Still fastened to the wall were chains and iron shackles, with a pair for both the hands and the feet of some unlucky individual. Alongside the wall was an old wooden chest. Lifting the lid revealed more shackles and some other iron implements, covered now with rust. A heavy chair rested on the wooden part of the floor.

One other item was curled in a corner, an ancient bullwhip of cracked and dried brown leather.

Suddenly the door to the chamber began to slam shut on us! I got to the entrance just in time to stop it. I pulled the door wide open, asked Amanda to hold it, and then brought in a broken cabinet from the outer room to prop the door open.

"You know what this is?" asked Amanda, her breathing hard and anxious.

"This is a torture chamber," I said. Amanda nodded and began to cry.

I felt the awfulness of it, too, but Amanda's tears puzzled me. "What is it?" I asked.

Amanda only cried. Then she surprised me even more. She moved over to the rough-hewn wall where the shackles and chains were fastened. She stood there and held her arms up to the open iron wrist-braces, and put her delicate ankles into the rusty leg restraints. She stood there for a long minute, her body bent to conform to the shackles. She looked vulnerable, a victim, like a crucified female Jesus. Amanda closed her eyes and cried terribly.

Suddenly I felt as if I was about to faint. I grabbed my gun tightly and surveyed the surroundings, getting a grip on my consciousness. I resolved that my mind would not desert Amanda in this moment, and I would keep my wits in focus.

I looked at her, as she posed in these old slave-shackles of another century, and all of a sudden her image changed before my eyes. Instead of modern clothes I saw her dressed in what seemed like burlap rags. And then her face changed – from white to black and then back to white again. My head was swimming but it did not feel like a hallucination. This was something else.

"Amanda!" I said, and ran toward her, and kissed her on the lips. I seemed to be kissing someone else at that moment, however. I took her in my arms and moved her away from the wall. She fell limply into my grasp. I remained alert, gun ready for action, and I gently carried her faint form into the room outside the door. Leaving our packs there downstairs, but taking

our guns and keeping one in hand, I picked up
Amanda and carried her outside and up the
steps of the old house. It was now less than an
hour before sunset. I nudged her awake in the
expectation we would soon leave.

"Amanda, my dear," I said quietly, "It's
gonna be dark soon, and we probably should get
going. Can you walk all right?" I asked.

Amanda's eyes opened and she exhaled
heavily. Her beautiful hair draped across my lap.
"Yes, I could walk," she said. "But we've got to
stay here tonight."

I felt a thud in my brain. I could not
think of something I had ever less wanted to do,
than remain here after dark in this old house
with its torture chamber. But Amanda was sure
this was the correct plan of action, and wherever
Amanda wanted to go or stay, my job was to be
by her side.

We were, indeed, about to spend a night
in hell so that we could catch a killer.

Night with a Demon

With only a short interval of daylight remaining, Amanda Poe and I got ready to spend the night at the abandoned Old Mansion. We decided to sleep on the house's main floor, in the large drawing room with the fireplace. Inspection by flashlight revealed that the chimney flue was clear enough to make it safe to start a fire.

I collected enough firewood from the dry Virginia woods to last the night, and before long the drawing room was warm and toasty – perhaps the first fire in the house in many decades. As I stood outside and looked up at the smoking chimney, I felt as if we were giving a signal to all the ghosts for miles around to come and visit us that night.

Inside of the house, Amanda laid out our sleeping bag and gear to make us as comfortable as possible. I made a last inspection of the grounds before the sun set, my gun in my hand as I peered into the growing dusk. I saw no one other than a young pretty-eyed doe in the woods. The sight of the doe cheered me up; she seemed a symbol of life and love, and I took my glimpse of this female deer as assurance from heaven that, whatever happened tonight, I would still be alive in the morning.

As dusk began to fall, I paid a last visit to the ground floor of the house with its torture chamber. There I saw another rat scurrying along. As I took a long look at those rusty shackles pinned to the wall, I wondered how many people had suffered in that room at the hands of a perverted master.

My tour of inspection complete, I joined Amanda Poe in the mansion drawing room, as the pink colors of twilight came through the wavy glass of the hundred-and-forty-year-old windows. We sat up against the wall tucked into my large sleeping bag, shoulder to shoulder, almost cuddling. It felt good to be so close to

Amanda. But this was too serious and dangerous of an evening to consider anything romantic.

"What went on downstairs?" I asked, "When you stood against the wall with your arms and legs in those shackles? You were in contact with the victims who suffered there, weren't you?"

"Yes, I was," she answered. "It was terrible, it was sad, but it was also very sweet. There were at least five victims that I can count. They were mostly young black women, dressed in rags, although one was a white woman dressed in a lot of old-fashioned finery. One of the young black women was really just a girl, thirteen or so. They'd all suffered there in a terrible way.

"But they seemed glad that we're here. They know we care about what happened to them, and that we want to listen. But I couldn't get much detail, there were so many voices. Plus *he* was there, too – I know nothing about him yet, but I sensed great, immense evil."

"You mean the killer?" I asked. "So is this the place where our three victims died? Will the killer come back here?"

"No, no," replied Amanda. "All this is very old. Whatever happened in this house and in that torture room downstairs, it's all ancient history. Those victims have been dead at least a hundred years.

"And the evil one I mentioned – he's been long dead, too. He's just a ghost now. But I think he knows something about the dead woman in the Louisa morgue, and the other murdered women. I think he – I mean his ghost – is going to come here *tonight*."

Amanda paused for a moment in silence, while I felt queasy and anxious. I wondered if she felt as I did.

"That ghost," said Amanda, "Is someone we *need* to see. I think he's the one who is preventing me from hearing the voices of our three murder victims. If we can get him to stop shouting and drowning out the other spirits, I think we can get somewhere."

"What are you thinking?" I asked. "Has some ghost from the past been reincarnated in a psychopath today? Has this ghost taken possession of someone's soul, and he's now killing again in a new body?"

"No," said Amanda. "I don't think it's anything that direct. Whoever is doing this killing today, is a person completely responsible for his actions. The ghost from the past is giving help and inspiration to the killer we're trying to find, but that killer is his own man. It's like a twisted teacher-student relationship. The ghost wouldn't be influencing our modern murderer unless the guy had the desire to rape and kill in the first place. The killer is getting encouragement and even ideas from the evil ghost of yesterday, but he's responsible for the murders he's committing even if the *way* he's murdering is influenced by the ghost.

"Take those shackles on the wall. All the bodies of our three modern victims were shackled with rusty iron before they died. The ghost we'll probably see tonight, he likely gave the idea of the shackles to the killer.

"But it's not the same shackles exactly?" I asked. "You don't think the murders took place here?"

"No."

"So probably the victims were just bound with some of the slave shackles that are always for sale at antique shops," I suggested.

"Right," said Amanda.

"Do you think that most serious crimes are partly inspired by demons or ghosts of dead criminals?" I asked.

"No," said Amanda, "I think it's pretty rare. Ghosts are all around us, but they actually don't interfere that much with living people. When a ghost does seriously influence life – even the ghost of a sadistic killer – there's always a reason for it. There has to be some kind of compulsion for the ghost to hang around, some kind of unfinished business that makes the ghost want to stay involved with the world."

She went on to explain further. "The most important reason that the dead try to influence or touch the living world, is for the sake of truth. Even the ghosts of dead criminals are passionately driven by the impulse to show the truth about themselves. When criminals die in a straightforward way, when their crimes are revealed, when they're openly killed while committing a crime – like the way you shot those two men to death the other week – or are executed for that crime, then the ghosts fade away.

"But when there is something hidden, something false, something that needs to be revealed to people still living, then the ghost is driven to continue to influence living people and events. This old house here has a lot of mysteries, which imply a strong reason for a ghost to remain active. Why was this place abandoned? Why is everybody in this county so afraid of it? What really happened in that torture chamber downstairs?"

"Well, this is Horton family land, probably," I noted.

"Right!" said Amanda. "And our patron and employer Dabney Horton knows something he didn't tell us, I'll bet that. If we're going to find out who's killing young women in Virginia, our first job is to find out the secret of this old plantation house."

"And," I added, "We probably can't ask Dabney directly, because he's either involved in this, or there's some aspect of family history he wants to hide." Amanda nodded her agreement. "But," I asked, "If Dabney's involved or wants to hide something, why did he hire us?"

"Something is out of his control," Amanda replied. "Any family like his has many secrets to hide, but I'm sure he doesn't want those young women killed. He's trying to play both ends against the middle, and of course it won't work that way."

"Because we're gonna find out the truth and make him 'fess up," I concluded.

"That's correct, partner," said Amanda. She put her head on my shoulder, and I enjoyed the feel of her body close by mine as night descended. By now there was only the light of the stars and the moon, and the glow of the embers in the fire.

Ghosts and murderers could come and try their worst, I thought. I was sure that Amanda and I would prevail.

* * *

It was night and it was quiet. There was only the crackling of the fire and the high-pitched chirping of woodland insects. Although it wasn't late in terms of hours, we were both tired, and given the simplicity of the setting it felt natural after a while to drift off toward sleep.

I began to forget about the strangeness of the place in which we rested: This old abandoned mansion with its century-old torture chamber. I began to forget about the murders, about the bodies dumped on the nearby roads, about a killer on the loose, and about the ghost of *another* creep from long ago, a ghost who seemed to be in our way.

As I dozed off it all seemed irrelevant, like a story that happened to someone else. I felt Amanda drop off to sleep next to me. I looked over at her sleeping face silhouetted in the firelight, and she seemed as pretty as ever. For a moment, there was just me and Amanda, and it felt beautiful.

After a while I, too, fell asleep. As I fell into the sleep zone I had a sense of falling, of being sucked in to somewhere.

And then I awoke. It was much, much later into the night. The fire had died down. I was sweating terribly, even though it was not very warm. My heart was pounding with fear and upset. Adrenaline was flowing. I could remember nothing from my time of sleep, I knew of no reason why I felt terror. But terror it was.

Near me, Amanda was curled up on the floor, as if she was preparing to defend herself from a large beast. She was breathing hard. I touched her shoulder, and I knew she was not awake. I walked over to put some logs on the fire.

The flames leapt high. The fireplace was like a part of hell, and it seemed that by stoking the fire I was giving a welcome to creatures from the inferno.

The flames were reflected in the old glass of the mansion windows. I looked at the reflections and then suddenly I saw a face in the flames. It vanished. It was visible just long enough to frighten me, and it disappeared quickly enough to leave a doubt whether it was anything more than a mirage.

Instinctively, I handled my guns, and moved closer to Amanda. I touched her shoulder again; she was rolled up in a ball facing away from me.

I closed my eyes and was pulled again into sleep.

All of a sudden I was awake again. Only now I was downstairs in the torture chamber, my nostrils recoiling from the awful smell and mustiness. The door to the chamber was closed, and the inside was lit by several thick yellow candles. I had not remembered seeing any candles there before.

I glanced around the room to look for Amanda; was she still upstairs, alone? Instead of Amanda, I saw a horrible sight: A young black woman, naked from the waist up, chained to the wall, her chest forward. Her back was bleeding from multiple whip-lashes and there seemed to be several knife-cuts as well. Blood dripped onto her crude skirt.

I tried to say something but my mouth wouldn't open. I tried to lunge forward to free the young woman but I couldn't move. I could only watch helplessly.

The face of the young victim turned to me. It was a very sweet face of a noble African heritage. Her eyes looked right at me. Despite her bleeding wounds, her face showed no sign of pain. Rather, her expression was an astonishing look of kindness and peace.

I felt myself lose consciousness. I swooned in the candlelight. I saw the young woman no more.

I awoke again. I was now on the floor of the torture chamber, lying there where I seemed to have collapsed. Candles were still burning, but they seemed to be different candles arranged in a different way. I was able to turn my head, and in turning I came to see, just inches away from me, the dead face of a young white woman, her eyes staring at me with the wide and empty stare of the recently murdered. Her face was spattered with blood. She was nude and lying in the dirt, a huge butcher knife with an ornamented wood handle lying partially buried in her chest.

I couldn't shout, I couldn't say anything, I couldn't move my hand or even my head anymore. I lay there for a long minute staring helplessly into the dead woman's face. Suddenly her face came alive! She looked at me. Her eyelids closed, and then in another second my eyes closed, too.

I awoke yet again and I was back up in the drawing room in the mansion, sitting on top of my sleeping bag. Amanda was awake, too, also sitting up. She held my hands in hers, and looked at me with an expression that was intent, aggressive, almost wild. Her hair was tossed and unruly, and her grip on my hands was tight.

She let go my right hand and raised her free arm before me, and then pointed to the large side window. As she began to point, I knew already I would see the ghost of an ancient murderer. I followed the direction of her finger with my eyes, until I saw the head and shoulders of a man with a dark and broad mustache, right outside the window, seemingly floating in the darkness. His clothes were of a style worn in the century past. He looked at us and there was no doubt he knew who we were.

I found that I was pointing my pistol at him, as if I was ready to shoot him right through the glass. He held up a hand, and then moved that same hand down and to the side, as if issuing a command; his eyes closed as his hand came down. I felt my eyes close, too, and I knew that Amanda was dropping unconscious as well. I remember clicking the safety on my gun back into place.

My eyes opened once more. I saw a young girl, barely a teenager, with hands and feet shackled, lying naked on a dirt floor; the girl was black and obviously a slave. She had been whipped and burned. There was a wound in her stomach that was bleeding. Her eyes rolled, her tongue hung out loosely. Another wound opened up in her chest, as if she was suddenly stabbed, though I could see neither the knife nor the attacker.

Candles burned in the background. I was back in the torture chamber, and once again I couldn't move. I heard laughter, but I could not see anyone other than the victim. There was another slash across the young woman's naked body, there was blood gushing, and another slash, and then another wound opened up, and then another. Blood drained onto the dirt, but the girl was still alive. She moaned and then screamed, horrible blood-churning screams that no one could hear other than the attacker and

116

me. Cuts appeared rapidly on the young woman's body, and more blood began flowing, but the victim still lived. Finally, blood spurted out from one of her wounds and flooded my own eyes and burned them, and I could see nothing. Then I was unconscious again.

Suddenly I was in Richmond, walking the ancient streets in my neighborhood near St. John's Church. It was over a hundred years ago, and men and women walked the streets in nineteenth century costumes. And then I saw him, the mustached man whose face I saw in the Old Mansion window. He was strolling the avenues of Richmond, walking stick in hand, looking at people on the street. I knew he was a killer, looking forward to mutilating his next victim.

I wanted to reach for my pistol, but I thought: The semi-automatic pistol has not even been invented yet. I did have another firearm on my person, however, a short old-fashioned 1850s percussion revolver. I began to draw my gun and the scene faded.

I know that after this last vision I slept a long time. My final awakening took place in the torture chamber downstairs, though throughout the night I had no recollection of going from one place to another.

When I awoke, I was sitting on the floor, with my right hand on my modern revolver. I looked up to see a single candle burning, and illuminated by the candlelight I saw my partner Amanda Poe, shackled to the wall, her eyes closed. I found I could move. I found I could speak. This seemed like no dream at all!

"Amanda!" I said. I undid her shackles, which were not locked.

"David! Oh, God, David!" she said.

"Are we here?" I asked. "Is this real?" I looked at my watch - nearly 5 a.m., not long before sunrise.

Amanda hugged me close. "Yes, David, this is real." Then she added, "Let's go back upstairs."

With gun in hand, I kicked open the entrance. The doors to the carriageway were open, letting in the moonlight. Amanda blew out the candle. "Fucking bastard," she said, and I knew she was talking to the ghost.

We both had our guns drawn as we went outside and up the house steps. "We don't need our guns for the ghost, do we?" I asked Amanda.

"We might run into a living creep who's carrying on his tradition," she replied.

Upstairs, in the drawing room, the fire had gone out, and our gear was thrown all over the place, but everything was there.

We took the big sleeping bag and went back out onto the porch of the mansion to await the dawn. I hugged Amanda and kept my arm around her. An owl hooted. Before long, the sun came up. A family of deer with wonderful cute young fawns greeted us along with the morning sun.

Amanda kissed me on the lips. "Thanks," she said. Our night's work had been done. We didn't say much. We would sort it all out later.

We gathered up our gear and went back toward my car. Once we crossed the stream that marked the border of the mansion grounds, we felt much better.

It was a night like I had never experienced before. Ghosts, visions, and a mysterious transportation from one place to another. I wondered what other bizarre things we would have to face before this murder case was closed.

Picture of a Killer

The morning after our night at the Old Mansion, Amanda said she needed to be alone for a while and that she would call me the next day. With all the weird goings-on of the night before, I was just as happy to leave the mysterious Amanda by herself and pretend I was a normal person again. Amanda asked me to do some research on the Old Mansion, and I told her I had a librarian acquaintance at the Virginia State Archives whom I could consult.

This acquaintance was actually an old girlfriend, Penny Schorr, whom I'd dated three years earlier for about six weeks. It was a brief relationship but a sweet one. It had ended for an odd reason.

Penny was a different kind of woman than the types I usually dated. She was intellectual, and usually dressed like a grown-up tomboy, always with big eyeglasses and very little make-up. There was a liveliness to her, a sparkle in her eye, that attracted me when I met her at an art gallery. I'm not an intellectual guy, but I do like bright conversation and I don't mind learning things from a pretty woman.

Penny taught me a lot about literature and culture, things I never knew. She made me wish I had read more books when I was in school. After a few weeks of dating her, I felt almost educated. For her part, Penny was a cute combination of smarts and absent-mindedness. She knew everything about the Civil War, but could never remember to check the oil on her car engine or even recall where she parked.

She seemed to enjoy the fact that I was a detective, and she told me all sorts of interesting stories from Arthur Conan Doyle to Agatha Christie. But what made us split up, was her feelings about the fact that I carried a gun. Somehow she didn't put the two things together at first; she didn't realize that my work as a detective required me to have a pistol as my constant companion.

The first night we slept together, she wound up staring at the holster I had placed on the floor. Finally, I hid the gun under my pants.

She talked about it frequently while we dated. She didn't seem afraid of guns, it was just that she was intellectually opposed to the idea. She didn't want to touch my pistol or handle it, or go to the shooting range with me. I always felt that if I had gotten Penny even once to go target shooting, and she found out how much fun it was, we would have overcome her objections and maybe developed a permanent relationship. But Penny always refused to go shooting.

I respect people who are opposed to guns or uncomfortable with them. For me, a gun is a tool. I carry a gun all the time, and I do it so well nobody even knows it's there. The concealed-carry shoulder holster is a completely natural part of my clothing. But I don't think guns are for everyone. They're just for people who have the right training and who knowingly accept the responsibility.

With Penny, however, it was the insurmountable hurdle to our relationship. Every other woman I've dated had accepted my carrying of a gun as part of my job, a tool of my trade. Sure, some of them were edgy about it at first, but I'd made a point of teaching firearms safety and basic shooting skills to every girlfriend who didn't already know these things, so that they could be comfortable with me and my pistol.

But not Penny. My gun-carrying broke up our relationship just as I was really getting to enjoy her. Although she never wore high heels or a short dress – she was always in flat shoes and blue jeans – I nonetheless came to think of her as wonderfully sexy. I loved to take off her blouse and pants, and then see her standing there, still wearing her glasses and little-girl-style underwear, talking profoundly about some topic while she put her body against mine and the lovemaking began.

Blue jeans and cotton panties, eyeglasses and ponytail. I always kept a soft spot in my heart for Penny. There was no rancor or nastiness in our break-up. She didn't even think it was wrong for me to carry a gun. "You need it," she admitted. "I'm just against them, it's just me. I can't be around deadly weapons every night." I argued and argued but her answer was still no.

I couldn't give up being a detective and Penny couldn't give up not wanting to be around guns. The night we broke up, it was Penny's idea to make love one last time. "Get undressed, I wanna touch it," she said.

"You mean my pistol? At last!" I replied.

"No, silly," she corrected me. "The *other* thing."

* * *

Penny and I still traded holiday cards, but I had not seen her since I caught a glimpse of her at a distance on the street last year. I did not tell her today that I was coming to visit; I wanted to surprise her.

I used my state police identification to enter the library stacks. The State Archives building is a huge institution that is not much used. A lot of books and documents that are rarely consulted are stored within its walls. A few exhibits on the ground floor have some traffic from students and tourists, and there are some rooms for the special usage of scholars and researchers in genealogy, but mostly the building is a big cavernous warehouse carefully tended by a few employees including my old girlfriend Penny.

I was told I'd find her on either the 5th or the 7th floor. I took my time walking through the building. Even though it was early afternoon, it was dark inside the Archive hallways. The building's large windows were filthy with external soot, and many of them were obscured by large bookcases. The rooms of the old building were filled with many rows of books and portfolios, on shelves that were stacked from floor to ceiling. Dim lights buzzed intermittently, and signs reminded you to turn off the reading-bulbs in each aisle to save energy.

It was all very gloomy. Rather a good place for a murder, I thought, if it weren't that librarians were such sensible and stable people.

I turned this way and that down the hallways, taking my time, and then I saw Penny. She was standing at a table where old brown-edged pamphlets were stacked in some kind of order. I could only see her back but I knew it was her. Faded jeans and a pretty clasp at the top of her ponytail, definitely Penny. I remembered the feeling of undressing her.

I knew it would be rude to touch her, so when I was a few feet away, I spoke.

"Hello, Penny," I said.

"That must be David Allan," she said, with a warm voice and smile, turning round to meet me. She touched my hands, and I felt some of the old warmth between us.

She asked me, "Are you tracking someone in these dark halls? This is a great place to hide if you get past the security out front."

"I'm tracking you," I replied.

"Well, I'm caught," she said. She looked at me through her big eyeglass lenses and I remembered kissing her. I felt nostalgic, as if Penny was part of younger days for me, when life was simpler, before I had shot any bad guys or seen any ghosts.

Penny was smart and talented. But she was not mysterious, not associated with darkness and death, like my new friend Amanda Poe.

We walked back to Penny's office, a big office that felt small because of the way that her desk and much of the floor and all of the wall shelves were crammed with papers and books. I told Penny I was working on a case, but I did not specify that it was the serial murders. I didn't think Penny was squeamish but I wanted to avoid unpleasant subjects with her.

I told Penny about the old abandoned plantation house in Louisa county and gave her the exact location. I said it was spooky, but I didn't tell her about the ghosts or the torture chamber. I said I wanted to learn everything about it, who owned it and lived in it in the 1800s and what's happened since then.

Penny said she'd be happy to collect the information for me. She told me to bring Chinese food for dinner, and come back this evening about 7:30, and that the security guard would let me in the back door. She said she had been planning to work late anyway.

"Are you seeing anybody?" she asked. Before I could answer, she added. "I've got a boyfriend. He's *crazy*," she affirmed, with what was clearly a mixture of consternation and affection.

"No, not really," I said, answering the question she had put to me about whether I was dating. "But I'm working with an interesting woman. Her name is Amanda Poe, and she says she's descended from the famous Edgar Allan."

"Amanda Poe!" said Penny. "I've heard about her. Very interesting woman, very mysterious. I always knew you had an unusual side to you, David."

I was taken aback. What did Penny mean?

"You know," she continued, "Edgar Allan Poe, *officially*, doesn't have any descendants. That's what most of the biographies say."

"Is Amanda Poe not telling the truth, is she just being colorful?" I asked.

"Oh no," said Penny. "I didn't mean anything like that. She might well be a descendant of Poe. There's always been stories about secret children of Edgar Allan Poe right from the beginning. And I know that some people – people whose opinions count – think that your friend Amanda is the real thing. It's considered polite not to press the issue, given that the lineage is not 'legitimate'. I wouldn't bug her about it until she volunteers to tell you exactly how she's related to Mr. Midnight Dreary.

"David," she added, "You still carry your gun always, don't you?"

"As we speak," I said, nodding affirmatively. Penny knew lots about history, but never read the daily paper or listened to the news. She probably didn't know I had shot two bad guys dead on the street the other week.

"Well, I'm glad," said Penny. "I still feel the same about them, but I'm glad you never compromised just for me." Penny was always able to confuse me.

I promised to bring some excellent Chinese food and see her this evening. I had no doubt that a good researcher like Penny would turn up something helpful.

* * *

Not knowing what else to do that afternoon, I took a walk around downtown Richmond and surveyed the grand buildings that grace this old city: The Old City Hall. The Governor's Mansion. The State Capitol designed by Thomas Jefferson. The White House of the Confederacy, where Jeff Davis led a four-year rebellion in favor of slavery and against the centralizing of national power. I wondered what a different place Richmond would be today, if the South had won the Civil War.

As I walked the streets, I thought as well about city life a few decades past, when people used to walk instead of drive, and when rich people preferred a big house *close* to downtown instead of far away from it.

I thought about how nice it was to live in Richmond, this comfortable, modest-sized, still gracious city, where artists and writers could still feel at home. I thought about Old Richmond a century and a half ago, when a brilliant young poet named Edgar Allan Poe walked these same

131

streets, and brooded upon the horrors of death and darkness.

Thoughts of death stayed with me as I strolled away from downtown across the Broad Street Bridge, toward the commercial area known as Shockoe Bottom. I walked past the art galleries and hair salons, the trendy new bars and restaurants, and toward the old cemeteries with their two-hundred-year-old headstones. An old stone gate, with the Star of David cut in its archway, marked the Jewish graveyard established in 1792. I thought of the Jews who came to this city when America was young so as to find freedom in its colonial society. These refugees from Europe would have brushed shoulders with Supreme Court Justice John Marshall and other men in knee breeches and silk stockings who had helped to found this nation.

Standing there in the Jewish graveyard, I took a deep breath of air and looked around me. The sun was shining and the weather was perfectly warm as I gazed upon the ancient and tumbled headstones from the half-forgotten past. Before these last few weeks, before I had met Amanda Poe, I had not realized one could so easily feel the spirit of death and gloom on a sunny day.

I walked over to another site of Richmond's history, a mass grave of horrible death that is poignantly unmarked. It's on the edge of a little-used and garbage-strewn parking lot. From the last curb, you can look down upon some rusty and abandoned railway tracks that lead to nowhere, ending in a tunnel entrance that is bricked up solid.

I scrambled down the grassy slope to the old railway roadbed for a better view. The closed tunnel entrance was a mere twenty yards in front of me. Carefully cut bricks filled the entranceway right to the top and all around the arch, excepting only a small hole near the middle where a small piece had fallen loose. The stone archway bore the chiseled inscription, "Richmond Terminus."

Beyond the entrance was a long railway tunnel nearly a third of a mile long. In 1924, when a train was in the tunnel blowing its whistle, there was an enormous collapse of the tunnel in three stages a few seconds apart. The train and its passengers were completely buried. Many more than a hundred people died inside. To this day there is no certainty as to the identity or final number of all whose lives ended there.

For a day and a night after the accident there were screams coming from inside the tunnel, but in the technology of the day it proved impossible to dig out the train or reach the victims. Eventually the screams died away and the rescuers gave up hope. The decision was finally made to leave the train and its corpses where they were.

To this day they remain: An old steam locomotive, tender and four cars: the engineer and his fireman; the conductor and his assistant; the gentlemen and ladies of the 1920s in their flapper-era finery; and the poorer white and black folks at the back of the train – all buried together in the rubble. They are buried where they died, and perhaps many of the skeletons still sit in the now-decayed seats where they sat in the final seconds of their life, forever a few minutes away from the now closed downtown train station that will await them for eternity.

I looked into the small hole in the tunnel entrance where the brick wall had fallen away. I heard sounds, first faint and then louder. The sounds were the screams of the men, women and children still inside. The screams were anguishing and blood-curdling.

But I knew that even if I organized an engineering commission to dig out that tunnel, there would be no one alive inside. The voices still calling from that train, were entirely and completely the voices of the dead.

* * *

I went home and made some coffee. There was no message on my answering machine from Amanda. She seemed indeed to be the kind of mysterious woman who will just up and disappear on you.

As evening fell I took a walk past Amanda's house; its windows were dark and silent. I wondered what kind of woman she really was, with all her strange powers. I mused on what it would be like to be involved with such a mystical feminine creature. Most of the

135

time she was human enough, but sometimes it was as if she was half-ghost herself.

Heading back toward the State Archives building where I was to meet Penny again, I walked through the intersection where I had shot the two men dead. Strangely, I was very happy and content with myself as I ambled across the street. Here was a place where I had *killed* two people, and I felt *wonderful*. I was fully enjoying the experience of my senses: The freshness of the air, the comfort of my clothes, the fluidity of my body as it moved. Life itself was a delight as I recalled surviving the gunfight. I felt no mental disturbance as an after-effect of the shooting. It was as if those righteous killings were a liberating experience.

Downtown Richmond was nearly deserted as 7:30 approached. There is something ghostly, in fact, about a modern downtown in the evening. The tall bank buildings and other office structures sit so silent and empty that they appear in mourning, as if their denizens have been annihilated.

I thought about how when I was a boy, "downtown" suggested fun and excitement.

Now, "downtown" is an idea that suggests fear and crime as much as anything. Most people on the street are harmless, of course, but I understood the fears of suburbanites who don't carry guns and who can't easily tell who is harmless and who isn't.

I picked up the Chinese food I promised to bring to Penny, and took it to the Archives building where the night guard let me in. The place was even spookier and gloomier than ever in the dusk. With most of the employees gone home, this big cavern of old books and papers seemed a place that ghosts might like to savor after dark. Virginia ghosts, in particular, might like to flit among the mementos of their past existence.

Moving through the building, I saw no one. I began to feel a little like I did the previous night at the haunted mansion in Louisa county. I recalled the face of the mustached man whom Amanda and I saw in ghostly visage through the Old Mansion window.

As I turned up the last flight of stairs to Penny's floor, I thought I could hear the clinking of chains, just like in the Old Mansion torture chamber. My hand reached for my gun, but I did not draw it.

I exited the staircase onto Penny's floor and felt a cold blast of air that seemed very strange, not coming from any vent nearby. I walked down an aisle till I could turn toward Penny's office; her door was open and the light was on. I let my gunhand fall back to my side. I walked toward her cubicle.

My lone footsteps echoed throughout the floor. In a few seconds I could hear Penny gently humming to herself, as I remembered she did when she was concentrating hard. I walked through her door without knocking.

She stood bent over a large table that was filled with yellowed books and pamphlets. Near one edge was a stack of photocopies obviously meant for me. She looked both thoughtful and sweet.

"You'll be proud of me," she said. "I've found some interesting stuff."

* * *

We sat down amidst the paper mess in Penny's office and she explained.

"The mansion in Louisa – is it this one right here?" She handed me a copy of an old woodcut engraving of a plantation house framed by a few trees. It was the very same house in which Amanda and I had just spent the night.

"That's it!" I said.

"Well, it was built in 1852 by some architects from England who toured the Old South in the 1840s and 1850s, building fine homes for the gentry of the era. It's currently owned by the famous Dabney Horton, through his real estate holding company 'The Colonel's Farm Ltd.', a company which was established in 1928. But the Old Mansion and the grounds surrounding it, and a lot of that stretch of Louisa County, have been in Horton family hands since just after the War." Of course when we Southerners speak of 'the War', we mean the War Between the States, 1861 to 1865.

Penny continued. "The people who first owned the house," she said, "Were Caleb and Abigail Jenkins, distant relations of the Hortons. They were not close by blood to the famous

Colonel Horton, but the Jenkins plantation is not all that far from the old Horton estate in Louisa.

"Those are the basic facts," she summarized, "But *then* things get interesting." Given my experiences of the night before, I didn't doubt that something bizarre had turned up.

"The Jenkins," said Penny, "Had only one child that lived beyond infancy, a man named Uriah who inherited the house in 1855 when his parents disappeared with a ship that sank on its way to England. That was the first unusual event.

"In the next few years there were several other disappearances. Several slaves vanished completely from the Jenkins plantation, and it was assumed they ran away up north on some underground slave-escape route that has not been documented otherwise. Then a woman disappeared from a neighbor's home, and finally Uriah Jenkins himself disappeared in 1859.

"Colonel Horton was executor of the estate, which was not settled until after the War ended. As the War continued, Colonel Horton gave the slaves squatter's rights to the plantation land, which many of their descendants still hold today. Uriah Jenkins' closer relations were killed or disappeared in the War, and by 1867, when the estate was settled, Colonel Horton was the owner.

"No member of the Horton family ever tried to live in the house, as far as I can tell. I found an article in an old *Virginia Intelligencer* from 1889, entitled "Ghosts at Jenkins' Mansion?", that said the Horton family tried to rent out the mansion, twice, to carpetbaggers from New York and Massachusetts, but that in both cases the new residents were driven away by strange events. The Horton family seems to have always refused to discuss the Old Mansion. They seem to have abandoned the place even though they continue to own it, which is strange given the money they spend on historical preservation of everything else connected with Colonel Horton and their family history."

Penny handed me the article on "Ghosts at Jenkins' Mansion?", which I read carefully and eagerly, looking for some connection to what I had seen the night before. The article, unfortunately, was short on detail, despite the teasing title. (Journalism obviously hadn't changed much in the last century.) There was a brief summary in the article about how all of the Jenkins and some of their slaves and one of their neighbors had mysteriously disappeared, but there were no hypotheses or conclusions about what had happened.

The article said that both of the families who had tried to rent the Old Mansion left Virginia in a hurry. There was second-hand gossip that one of them had "seen things move and fly in the night", and the other had "seen sights no human being should ever face". The article had noted that the Hortons were honorable enough to refund in full the rent that had been paid.

"Anything more on Uriah Jenkins?" I asked. "I'm still working on him," said Penny. "I've found one picture, an old daguerreotype. I reproduced it with the high-resolution copier in the art department. You can have the copy."

It was *him*, the ghost we had seen last night in the Old Mansion window! What a horror I felt, to see that face again! The dark mustache, the piercing look: It was him indeed, the face of the menacing ghost whose vision I had shared with Amanda Poe.

I now had no doubt. The spirit world was real, and Amanda was my guide to the world beyond death.

The adrenaline rushed within me, and I felt something like fear. This strange man of a hundred and forty years ago, I was sure, was somehow connected with the recent murders of three Richmond women.

"He looks spooky, doesn't he?" said Penny, in all innocence.

"For sure," I agreed. "Tell me anything you can about him."

"This Uriah Jenkins, he doesn't seem to be well connected to the social world of his day. The Jenkins' names are not often on the society and party lists of the time. My guess is that they were somewhat private people.

"They rented a townhouse in Richmond, too, on Twentieth Street. Here's the address. First his parents and then Uriah himself would have spent some time in Richmond on business, trading farm goods, slaves and horses."

"Any more information on the slaves who disappeared?"

"No," said Penny, "That would be hard to come by. A lot of slave-holding records were destroyed in the shame after the War, and I'm still looking even to find their names. There almost certainly wouldn't be any pictures. In fact, we don't even have any pictures of Uriah's parents.

"How about the woman who disappeared, the Jenkins' neighbor?"

"Oh, yes! We do have something on that, that was actually a major scandal. All the chivalrous men of the time went out looking for her. She had disappeared while horseback riding; her horse came back alone the next day.

"Her name was Elizabeth Wallenford, and she was young and pretty. We do have a lovely small photograph of her, taken just before she vanished."

Penny opened an old book that had a locket-sized photo of the long-dead Elizabeth. The face looked familiar, and indeed within a couple of seconds I knew why: It was a face I had seen last night, the blood-splattered face of a dead woman with eyes wide open, lying on the floor of the torture chamber in the Old Mansion.

The truth of my visions last night were now doubly proved. Even more profound was that I felt touched by the spirit of this dead Elizabeth. I felt a certain warm glow as I thought of this poor murdered woman now deceased for well more than a century. Her spirit seemed to be glad that, at last, someone living knew not only her fate but also her name.

"Bettie," I said out loud, somewhat involuntarily. I felt sure I had just voiced the nickname of the long dead woman.

"Well," said Penny, a bit startled by my informal reference to the woman in the picture, "Maybe if she were alive today, maybe the two of you could be friends."

"Maybe so," I agreed, smiling. I felt again the warmth within me of being touched by Elizabeth's spirit.

"That's just about what I have," concluded Penny. "I don't think there's much more in the records. Is this helpful?"

"Oh, yes," I said. "You've been terrific."

"That's what you used to say when we made love together," she replied.

I nearly blushed, but I didn't say anything. We opened up the food I had brought and warmed it in Penny's office microwave. We talked no further of the plantation house in Louisa, and Penny didn't ask me about why I wanted the information – as if she knew there was something horrible at hand.

It was already dark when we got ready to leave the Archives building. Penny called her boyfriend to come pick her up outside the back door. Before we reached the stairway she grabbed me and held me at arm's distance. "You know I'll never forget you," she said.

"Me neither," I answered. Our relationship was a memory sweet to my heart. "Any regrets?" I asked, a little boldly.

"Sometimes I wish'd you'd been a bit more aggressive in your lovemaking," she replied. She kissed me. I was startled by her statement, and intrigued by what she meant. The last twenty-four hours had been full of surprises.

I walked with her downstairs, and I waited with her for her boyfriend. He arrived within two minutes, and she waved a cheerful goodbye. From the light of the streetlamps I could see her looking at me over the edge of the car seat. I could feel us both wondering about what might have been.

Even when it's brief, even when it's over, there's a sweetness to any true romance that is not forgotten.

Slave Quarters

The next morning, while I was out at the grocery store, Amanda left a message on my answering machine telling me that I should meet her at her house at 4 o'clock that afternoon. She didn't say what was on her agenda, but she did leave me an enigmatic caution: "Don't do anything else about the case until I see you. Please, David, I mean it."

So I stayed indoors and puttered about the house till afternoon, and then I strolled over to Amanda's. I had very much *missed* her in the day and a half we'd been apart.

As she opened the door she seemed glad to see me. She wore a flattering nearly-sheer skirt with black tights underneath. She looked rested and refreshed.

I thought about giving her a hug. We'd kissed the other night, but that was in the strange circumstance of the haunted mansion. I had no clue as to the possible course of our relationship, so for the moment I decided to be professional and restrained.

"Where have you been, partner?" I asked, keeping a respectful distance.

"I've been a bird," she said, in a tone that was warm but serious. "I've been flying, here and there, trying to be wise like the wind. But I'm back now," she said, touching my arm. She looked at me with her large, dark eyes, eyes that sparkled with affection.

I did not ask the meaning of her strange words, and I decided I wouldn't press her as to where she had been in the last thirty-six hours. For all I knew, maybe she *had* been a bird, and maybe she and that stone raven above the doorway had both taken flight together.

"Tell me what you've found," Amanda said, as we sat down in her living room.

I told her everything I'd learned from Penny yesterday, and I showed Amanda the picture of Uriah Jenkins, the owner of the Old

Mansion who had disappeared mysteriously in 1859.

"That's him, all right, that's the ghost who's been blocking us," Amanda said, matter-of-factly. "He still looks the same, doesn't he?" she asked, referring to our mutual sighting of Uriah's ghost the night before last.

I stared at Uriah's picture, trying to figure out what was the connection between this man who disappeared in the 1850s and three women who were just murdered in 1990s Richmond. "Amanda, what is going on ?" I asked. "I need you to explain this to me so I can understand."

"Don't you see?" replied Amanda, as if it were all so obvious. "Uriah Jenkins is the ghost we saw at the mansion. Even though he died more than a hundred years ago, he's very active now, *today*, and *he* is the one who's interfering with my contact with the spirits of the three murder victims. He's protecting the killer, he's keeping us from finding the truth. But now that we know who he is, we can beat him."

I didn't say a thing. The wheels in my brain were turning double-time while Amanda explained further.

"Your friend Penny said there were a number of people who disappeared in the 1850s. Remember all the things we saw at the Old Mansion?" How could I forget! "It all adds up. The missing slaves. The Wallenford woman who was Uriah's neighbor. The torture chamber downstairs in Uriah's house.

"David, Uriah Jenkins was the *killer* of all those people. That's who and what we saw in our dreams and visions the other night. We saw the victims, and we saw the killer, in a string of murders that took place before the Civil War."

I sat there thinking for a moment, and Amanda just silently watched me. Then I asked, "But what about Uriah? Why did he disappear, too? Did he kill himself in disgust? Or maybe he wasn't the killer, and was just another victim – is that possible?"

"No," said Amanda, with absolute assurance. "Uriah is *the devil* – I tell you, he's the devil! What happened to him, though, is something that we still have to discover. Something unusual *did* happen to him, and the secret of Uriah's disappearance has stayed hidden ever since 1859. That's why the Old

Mansion is still haunted. And more importantly, that's why Uriah's ghost is still around today causing trouble.

"Sometime recently," Amanda continued, "Somebody who is alive today in Virginia, who is himself an evil, bad person, has come into contact with the ghost of Uriah Jenkins. Uriah's evil spirit was probably the final catalyst in encouraging this person to become a murderer.

"The crimes that Uriah committed in the 1850s have become the model for the killer who is murdering women right now. This killer has dreams of Uriah just like we had visions in the Old Mansion. For you and me, David, those visions are nightmares. But for the killer, those dreams are a fantasy he wants to make real. And he is perverted and evil and determined enough to find a way to make his sick desires into a real and *horrible* session of torture and death.

"The killer is driving his victims' bodies out to Louisa county to get closer to that fantasy, to feel nearer to Uriah's ghost. The killer may never have been to the Old Mansion and maybe even doesn't know he's driving dead bodies to Uriah's old plantation. But he does know that it feels good to his perverted mind to take those cut-up corpses of young women out to that place in the country where Uriah Jenkins had his old homestead.

"Uriah's ghost, for all his evil, still wants the truth to come out about himself. He's continuing to inspire murders today because he *wants* the arrow of investigation to point backwards in time. He *wants* us to discover what happened to him. That's why he's screaming in our brains every time we try to listen to the spirits of the three victims, who were murdered by a killer inspired by Uriah. He doesn't care about the killer or the victims; what he does care about is exposing his identity and the truth about his time on earth. Encouraging a serial killer is the satanic method by which Uriah's ghost has chosen to reveal himself.

"David, we have *got* to finally solve the mystery of the Old Mansion. We've got to find out what really happened to Uriah, or we may never catch the killer who's walking the streets right now. When we solve the mystery of how Uriah Jenkins disappeared, and bring that to the light of day, his voice will grow quiet and we can focus on the modern killer that we have on the loose."

It sounded crazy, but it made a kind of sense too. Amanda certainly knew more about the spirit world than I did, and in my heart I felt she was right about how to catch the killer.

"What about Dabney Horton?" I asked. "Couldn't he help us with something? With the Old Mansion being in his family and all, wouldn't there be some old legend or story passed on from his grandparents that might give us a clue?"

"Oh, definitely," said Amanda. "Old Dabney knows something. He knew something the day he hired us, something he wasn't telling us. But there's no point in talking to him. If he had wanted us to know, if he felt he *could* tell us, I'm sure he already *would* have told us. Dabney might have paid us to come into this case, but Dabney Horton is probably as much of an obstacle now as anything else."

"Think we should ask him anyway? You can often learn something by the way a guy evades a question."

"No," said Amanda. "We're awfully close now, and if Dabney senses we're on to him, he could get in our way. Let's try to get the answer ourselves. I know how we should start."

Although I was older than Amanda and had more experience as a detective, today I was certain I was the junior partner in this investigation. "You beckon and I obey," I said.

"I *like* that," said Amanda, with girlish glee. "Let's spend the evening at Slave Quarters."

* * *

Slave Quarters is an unusual and controversial complex of art galleries, shops, restaurants and a disco. It had been open now for about two years. The large Slave Quarters building is in Richmond's Shockoe Bottom, southeast of downtown along the bend of the James River.

Originally built in 1832, the now-renovated structure was literally what its name suggests: A holding pen for trading in human flesh. Slave Quarters was the principal venue in

Old Virginia's capital city for the buying and selling of black men, women and children.

Slave Quarters was central Virginia's slave-trade headquarters until the Civil War, when it was commandeered as a prison for Union soldiers. Several famous Union spies were hanged in its courtyard in full view of the other prisoners, the chains of their hand and leg irons clanging noisily as their bodies dropped through the trap door at the end of a stout rope.

After Reconstruction, the building functioned once again as a sort of "slave quarters" in that it was the jail for poor blacks from central Virginia. Just before World War I, several hangings took place there again, on the theory that it was a useful example to have black felons hanged in the sight of the other black prisoners.

By the 1920s, the deteriorating condition of the facility precluded its continuing use as a prison, and the building was largely abandoned. In the 1960s, the building was briefly opened as a museum, but the finances were not in place to keep it open.

Finally, in the 1990s, the ongoing development of the Shockoe Bottom precinct made it logical to develop the old building, and many local artists were eager to use the small partitioned spaces that once functioned as holding pens for small groups of slaves who were destined for sale or transfer.

It was decided not to hide the building's past, but rather to use its history as part of its modern identity. Provision was made for exhibit areas on the practice of slavery and its horrors, but the whole project remains controversial. Some critics felt that it is wrong to put trendy eateries, bars and discotheques in the Slave Quarters building because it trivialized the grim reality of black servitude in America. The contrary argument was that only the commercial success of Slave Quarters provided the finances to support the Slavery Museum and Memorial within its walls.

Controversy aside, the project was an unqualified economic success. Many of Richmond's best artists show their work in the Slave Quarters galleries, and the mix of shops and cafes and restaurants and the dance club, proved to be an effective commercial formula. Slave Quarters was active every night, and thoroughly mobbed on weekends.

And tonight was Saturday night.

* * *

Amanda and I got to Slave Quarters about seven o'clock – still early for serious partygoers, and yet there was a full throng in the building's central atrium with its gurgling fountains. The restaurants were doing good business but we managed to find a table. We both ordered steaks, and shared a bottle of red wine.

"What do you think?" asked Amanda. "Is it wrong to turn an old slave market into Richmond party central?"

"Something about it seems tacky," I answered. "I wonder what the slaves who were bought and sold here would think about it now. Plenty of their descendants seem to be here having a good time." I looked down the atrium and I saw the faces of many African-American men and women, happy to join the weekend partying with everybody else.

Amanda sat quietly for a moment, her eyes looking upwards as if she was listening. "I don't think the people who were slaves mind we have a good time now in this building," she said, "As long as we *remember*. I'm glad the Slave Museum and Memorial is here."

"Do you think the ghost of Uriah Jenkins might be here, too?" I asked. "And how about the killer we're looking for – Is he maybe out there, right under our nose, sitting at a bar stool, contemplating his next murder?"

"I think Uriah's around," answered Amanda. "His work would have brought him here a lot in the 1840s and 1850s. But I don't feel anything very specific. We'll have to spend some time, take a closer look. This might have been the place that Uriah and our murderer connected with each other, but we're going to have to scratch around before we know that."

Dinner was pleasant and the wine softened our moods. It was partly work but it also felt like a date. And I felt very special to be the escort of the exotic Amanda Poe.

* * *

After dinner, our first stop was the Slave Memorial and Museum, which was open whenever the Slave Quarters complex was open. Even late on Saturday, the serious-minded could look at some exhibits on the history and practice of slavery.

We paid the two-dollar admission to the security guard, and entered inside of the thick glass doors. It was strangely quiet within. The Museum was well-insulated against the noise and hubbub of the shops and restaurants and the traffic in the hall.

The first thing you see inside the Museum is a life-size sculpture of a man, woman and child in rags. The clothes of the two adults are torn, and their bare backs are scarred by whiplashes. The plaque beneath has the simple inscription, "For All Those Who Suffered and Died in Servitude, 1607-1865".

On the wall nearby is an enlarged photograph of a black man in ripped clothes, his back bloody from a whipping, hanging from a crude gallows. The caption beneath said, "The last slave known to have been executed in Virginia. Known simply as Jeremiah. Hanged for inciting other slaves to rebellion in 1863." The photograph is clearly authentic. A simple, powerful, awful picture that summarizes the horror of American slavery.

Amanda and I toured the Museum in respectful silence. I had been there before, but the exhibits moved me just as much now, seeing them for the second time. Amanda seemed an almost angelic presence by my side. Her face glowed with respect and compassion, and I knew that she felt a deeper bond than most people to the dead slaves of long ago.

There were many exhibits of authentic items connected with slavery. Bill of sale documents, and written instructions for the management and punishment of slave labor. Tools they had used, clothes they had worn, utensils by which they ate and drank. There were whips that had beaten them, chains that had bound them, ropes that had hanged them.

One part of the museum was especially personal for us. The Slave Museum had been built around a section of the building wall that remained in its original crude condition. This wall surface had been constructed in 1832 with sets of shackles and chains embedded in it, instruments that were used to bind slaves who were ready for sale in this building's early era.

What was especially touching was that there were two height levels of hand shackles. Some were at a higher level for adults, but in every position there were additional small shackles not far above the ground, such as were useful to hold children. My heart went out to the memory of the young boys and girls who had waited in these shackles to be sold. What a terrible crime was the institution of slavery!

The shackles here on the wall reminded Amanda and me of the torture chamber in the Old Mansion we had visited in Louisa. As we stared at the shackles now, Amanda grabbed my arm. We both could feel the deep connection between this place and that place, between the one horror and the other.

Amanda didn't have to tell me. I *knew* that Uriah Jenkins, the pervert and murderer of the 1850s, had been *here*, in this building, in this slave marketplace, perhaps standing in the very spot that I was standing now. Perhaps he had looked at some poor young woman held in these shackles and thought: *Here is a woman I can buy and use, not just for work, but also as an object for rape, and torture, and sadistic bloody murder.*

Suddenly I saw Uriah's face again in my mind. Amanda and I looked at each other. We didn't say a word. We knew, we both knew. *He* was here.

* * *

The Museum made no attempt to smooth over the horrors of slavery, but it did provide a balanced view of life under servitude. Some of the masters were kind or at least decent, and some of the slaves lived reasonably comfortable lives. In some cases, slaves had a materially better life before the Civil War than they did afterwards, when freedom sometimes meant abandonment and starvation.

One glass case contained an old Virginia law book open to the sections governing treatment of slaves, who did have some limited rights under Old Southern law. There was a point of abuse beyond which even a slaveowner could not go. The sign on the exhibit stated that it was part of the "chivalric code" of Southern gentlemen to keep the treatment and punishment of slaves within the legal limits.

These were limits that Uriah Jenkins had obviously crossed in that torture chamber downstairs in his mansion. The exhibit stated that, "Excessive abuse of slaves was a punishable offense under state laws in the Old South, although in practice there were few legal actions taken against slaveowners." There was certainly no record of legal action against Uriah Jenkins, or my friend Penny would have found it.

As one completes the circuit through the Museum, the last stop is the bookshop, presided over this evening by a young man who turned out to be the Assistant Curator, a learned graduate of the University of Virginia. Amanda asked this Dr. Maxwell if it was unpleasant to work here every day amid these sad signs of the horrible past.

"It's *meaningful* work, that's how I'd put it," he replied. "Even though I'm an African-

American, I don't focus so much in my mind on the horrors of slavery, but more on the whole picture of slaves as people. In my own historical work I study the daily lives of slaves, and I find their lives are composed of the same essentials as our own. People are born, they learn things, they work, they play, they get sick, they suffer, and eventually they die. The horrors of slavery are a part of their lives, but to me, slaves are first of all just people, *my* people, my own ancestors.

"I've gotten so close to them," Dr. Maxwell continued, "That I no longer see them as just victims. After all, society today is full of victims, too, who are just victimized in newer and more modern ways. To me, the slaves of North America were generally simple but courageous people who adapted with a lot of grace to a very difficult situation. I'm proud of them. I love them. And I feel I honor them by helping the world not to forget them."

Amanda and I said good-bye to this elegant young scholar and we went on our way. Just next the doorway out of the bookshop was a picture of the interior of Slave Quarters in its final years as an active slave auction house, circa

1857. The old building was recognizable even though the modern installation of upscale restaurants and shops was more than a century in the future.

In that old photo, the slave marketplace was thronged, with the white men buying and selling, and the shackled black men, women and children being paraded about as merchandise. The crowds in the picture were blurry from movement, and I could not help wondering the whereabouts of Uriah Jenkins when the picture was taken.

* * *

Next door to the Museum was a Slave Art boutique, which sold detailed and excellent reproductions of arts and crafts that had actually been created by slaves and former slaves. There were crafts, jewelry and even some paintings, of an inventiveness and quality that was entirely remarkable considering that some of the originals had been created in slave conditions. The human spirit can still express beauty even under the tragic circumstance of being owned and dominated by somebody else.

Amanda and I spent several hours in the Slave Quarters complex amid the increasingly large and growingly inebriated Saturday night crowd. We hoped to fall upon some hint, some insight into our murder case, although we knew this wouldn't be easy.

One spot that rang some bells for us was the Old South General Store, which sold genuine antique items from the Confederacy and Antebellum periods. Near the usual quantities of bullets and buttons was a box of allegedly genuine slave shackles and chains, all appropriately aged and rusty. They were rather expensive, but the clerk told us that they sold well. We also learned that staff at the store turned over frequently because of the low wages and cranky ownership. The clerk said that he, too, was planning to quit as soon as he found a better job.

It was possible that the killer of the three recently murdered women had bought his shackles of death here at this shop. At the same time, the amount of floor traffic in the store plus the frequent staff change-overs made it just about impossible we could trace the killer through this kind of purchase.

As we left the shop, Amanda said, "I can feel the fresh bloodstains. I think the killer bought his toys *here*." Somberly, I looked back at the store and the many people moving through its aisles. I tried to paint a mental image of the murderer, but I only drew a blank.

Another spot in the Slave Quarters complex that earned a few minutes of our attention was a sex-toy boutique called The Penalty Box, run by a hairy-chested man with no shirt and a leather vest, wearing a policeman-style cap. At least half of its goods were sado-masochism related, leather whips and bondage items, and chains and shackles that were "grand spanking new", rather than the rusty items down the corridor at the antique store.

I took one of the brochures referring customers to the "Different Strokes Club", which advertised "Safe and Wild Sex for the Nineties" under discreet circumstances. The proprietor smiled at the two of us, and I realized that Amanda and I looked the part, she in her black tights and heels and flimsy skirt, and me with my self-assured and interested survey of the S&M paraphernalia.

"Would you want to whip me?" asked Amanda, within playful earshot of the other customers.

"Only when you deserve it!" I replied, and I took her arm and we exited the store.

"See you soon!" said the shop manager, confidently.

Amanda and I laughed as we walked down the hall. We did not find anything else at Slave Quarters which we could consider as a potential lead or clue, though we did feel it was a productive evening.

On our way out we peeked into the dance club. "I like to dance sometimes," said Amanda. She looked so beautiful, I wanted to dance with her. But tonight was not a night to drink and play. We had a murderer to catch.

We went our separate ways home and resolved to meet again the next morning. Tomorrow would be the day Amanda and I almost got killed.

Death in the Morning

I got up early on Sunday and went out to the local café for coffee and a croissant. Sunday mornings on Church Hill are especially beautiful. Traffic is light, the church bells ring their ancient songs, and people dressed in their best clothes gently make their way to and from services at St. John's and the other houses of worship.

I don't go to church myself – as a single man it feels funny going to church with all those families and children – but my visions of ghosts in these last few days made me think about religion this morning. I wasn't sure what I believed about God, but I sure knew now there was something out there, a world of spirits beyond this earthly plane.

I had just gotten back to my townhome when Amanda called me on the phone. She was eager to go to work. She suggested we get going early to visit the location of the house that Uriah Jenkins had rented in Richmond. That address was now on the edge of some drug-dealer-infested housing projects, and Sunday morning was the safest time to visit the area at leisure. I agreed this made sense. Even detectives who carry guns are careful about when they visit bad neighborhoods.

I picked up Amanda in my car and she was a sight to behold. She was wearing a combination of black and royal blue colors, with a beautiful necklace and a shiny pair of earrings showing amid her long tresses. She had a light jacket concealing her gun and spare ammo. She was lethally armed and fetchingly beautiful.

As we pulled away from the curb in front of Amanda's porch, both of us were quiet, enjoying the early morning view of the wonderful old houses in our Church Hill neighborhood. I thought about how unsafe these streets could be late at night. And then, in a curious anticipation of fate, I mentally counted up the rounds of ammunition that the two of us were carrying on our Sunday morning excursion. My full-sized pistol held fifteen rounds in the magazine. Even after loading one round in the firing chamber, I didn't "top off" the clip with an extra round, so as to reduce stress on the magazine springs. Since the gunfight, I had gone back to the habit of carrying two extra clips of ammunition on my belt with fifteen rounds each, so I had forty-five cartridges total.

Amanda had told me the first evening we'd met, that with her compact pistol that held only eight rounds in its magazine, she did top off the clip after loading the firing chamber. So she had nine rounds live in her gun, and she said she always carried two extra eight-round clips as well, for a total of twenty-five rounds in all.

That meant that Amanda and I had seventy shots between us of the deadliest ammunition we could buy. I smiled at the thought of what seemed like excessive firepower concealed beneath her clothing and mine.

My musing on quantities of ammunition is something I should have understood as a premonition. All those extra bullets were about to save our butts.

* * *

The car that I drive is a big oversized hunk of V-8 American technology, a Mercury Grand Marquis, the same model used by many government agencies as a police cruiser. Half for intimidation and half because I like the style, I dress my car up like an unmarked cop car: Fat blackwall tires, a searchlight by the driver's door, and several antennas on the back window and hood. The look of the car, and my own somewhat square appearance, give many people the quick illusion that I am some sort of policeman.

The truly knowledgeable will see that I am not a cop, however. I have private-citizen license plates, not state plates; I have the plush car interior they'd never allow a cop to ruin; I have a car phone antenna but no car phone (the phone was repossessed when I didn't pay the bill); and my three antennas don't match the configuration of any law enforcement agency known around these parts.

I think the cop-car appearance of my vehicle helps avoid trouble, although I know that my car's look might also invite an attack from punks who enjoy harassing the fuzz. In any case, when the shooting started on this Sunday morning, the appearance of my copper brown pseudo-police-car did not prevent one of the wildest shooting sprees this city has ever seen.

* * *

Our visit to the old Uriah Jenkins townhouse site began normally. The house number on 19th Street was just across from the Manson Court projects, where good people lived cheek-by-jowl with some very nasty drug dealers, and where many of the visitors were desperate drug buyers.

These buyers and sellers of narcotics managed to shoot one or two of their number dead in public at least several times each season, with the occasional maiming or murder of an innocent child or bystander. It was always the same afterwards: Dead bodies on the grass or in the street, and a hundred people milling around, none of whom ever admitted to seeing anything.

I have no unusual fears of bad neighborhoods. I'm a pretty tough egg, and obviously, so was Amanda. Act smart and look tough and the odds are in your favor – We both knew that. Amanda and I went about our business without any thought the morning would end even in an incident, much less a heap of bodies.

There was no building standing at Uriah's old townhouse address. In fact, an entire row of houses here had been torn down long ago. Further down the street, a few structures on this block were still standing, the first of them with a caved-in roof. The next one in the row had smashed-in upper windows, an open front door, and sleeping emaciated derelicts on the stoop. The generic look of a haven for crack cocaine.

We parked in front of one of the now-empty lots where houses had been demolished. A few nicely dressed ladies were across the street strolling toward church. A lone wino was sleeping in the street, and a couple of ornery-looking but not immediately threatening characters stood nearby. In other words, it looked like a normal Sunday morning near the projects.

The lot that was once the site of Uriah's Richmond residence had the remains of an old building foundation and a portion of an old brick fireplace. Not far behind the fireplace rubble was an illegal dumpster, abandoned here and overflowing with trash. Garbage was strewn about the entire lot as well.

So there we stood, on the site of a house now fallen down, a house once rented by the Jenkins family in the 1850s. We were here looking at the remains of a fireplace probably used by 19th century slaveowner Uriah to warm himself when he visited town to buy and sell human flesh, and where he perhaps mused upon the women he would kill.

We had visited the country plantation house now haunted by Uriah's ghost. Was this garbage-strewn lot haunted as well?

I knew the significance of where we were, but strangely I felt nothing. Throughout a lot of the last week I'd been able to feel and see some of the things Amanda Poe was perceiving. I'd shared in her dreams, her visions, her nightmares. But here, looking at this pile of rubble and garbage, at the bricks of an old broken-down fireplace covered now with soda cans and wind-blown fast food wrappers and someone's used underpants, here I felt nothing. I felt no sense of the supernatural, no sense of history or the past. It was just the ordinary here and now, junk and trash on an empty lot in a bad neighborhood.

But Amanda was having a different experience. *She* was feeling the history of where we were. I could see she was experiencing Uriah's ghost. Her face was angry, serious, disgusted. Not disgusted at the garbage merely, but disgusted at something else more serious, something she was seeing and feeling in the realms of the spirit.

"Here is the place," Amanda said, with solemn assurance. "We've at last begun to find our killer. Here is the place the killer met Uriah."

Of a sudden Uriah's nasty 19th century face came into my mind, and then it disappeared again. For a second I had felt myself in the past. Then, I was once again in the present, once again just a man standing in an empty lot by the edge of the projects.

I didn't doubt Amanda's notion about this place connecting two killers a century apart from one another. I didn't know how Amanda arrived at this astounding conclusion, but then, I didn't have Amanda's unusual powers of seeing into the world beyond, powers which had already been well proven. My role was just to patiently wait for Amanda to figure out as much as she could from the spirits hovering upon this old plot of Richmond city ground, after which I would be glad to leave this seedy neighborhood.

And then, something happened. There was nothing external at first, just some sudden strange feelings. Time began to slow down, just like it had that evening when the two hoodlums pulled up in front of the young college student and I had to shoot them down.

I looked at Amanda, and she knew it was happening, too. Her look was wild, wild like I had never seen her before. Amanda had one foot in the next world, and one foot in this one, and both worlds were going crazy.

Time slowed down, and then I could swear it stopped. I was still thinking and still breathing but I couldn't move. Amanda was frozen and pale white, like a statue.

Then time began to creep along again, at a tiny fraction of its normal pace. The next two minutes would seem like hours, and at the end of those two minutes eight people would lay dead or dying.

* * *

The remains of Uriah's old townhouse were part of a row of vacant lots, at the end of which stood the two men whom I had noticed upon our arrival. They were mean-looking types, later identified as drug dealers, but they had been calm and casual about our presence while we did our initial survey of the grounds of Uriah Jenkins' old city home. These two men were about thirty-five yards away when the gunfight started.

At first nothing seemed to happen. There was a pause in time, like in a science fiction movie, and the entire neighborhood was silent except for the gentle rustle of a morning breeze. It was an eerie silence, a cold silence, the silence of men and women about to die.

Three things started to occur almost at once, but all in slow motion. A chubby, scruffy man came around the corner from the area of the houses that were still standing at the end of the block. He wanted to talk to one of the two drug dealers. He was speaking very loudly; not exactly shouting, but nonetheless angry. His words were strong, his tone forceful, but his look was that of a rabid animal. He had a twitch of vulnerability that marked him as a victim.

Out of the corner of my eye, I could see a car pulling up near to where my car was parked on the street, in the opposite direction from the three men in the argument. The newly arrived vehicle had three people in it, people whom I sensed were prepared for violence. One of them was a woman.

At that moment I wished that Amanda and I were in *my* car and driving away from this

181

scene. My car was only twenty yards away, but it might as well have been in a parking lot in Chicago for all the good it was doing me at that distance. I already knew that if Amanda and I tried to get to my car, we would never make it alive.

A third menace emerged from the housing project across the street. Three men, very much a gang, emerged from a second floor doorway and hurriedly walked down some wooden stairs, in the direction of the argument underway between the chubby man and the two drug dealers.

I understood the situation immediately. It was destined for gunplay, and Amanda and I would be caught in the crossfire. The chubby man was backed by the group in the car, and the two drug dealers were backed by the gang from the project. Both groups of antagonists would assume we were with the other side.

It seemed inevitable there would shortly be blood spilled and some bodies on the ground, and it would take some luck for Amanda and I to both come out unscathed. As of yet no guns were visible, but a deadly firefight was only seconds away. I remember thinking that I hoped it would be me who was shot and not Amanda. I looked at her and she knew, too, that death was coming toward us. And not only was death en route; death was driving a special shuttle bus for the event.

As I looked at Amanda I saw her close her eyes for a brief half-second, as if to give herself time for a quick telegram to the world of the spirits. There was no color in her at all; she was white as a hospital sheet. But when her eyes opened, there was steely resolve and the flame of courage in her face.

Seeing her like that, I felt my own aggressive passions shoot up within me. Almost perversely, I was thrilled and excited about the game to be played, and I was absolutely confident in trusting my partner in the gunfight to come.

I would never have chosen to be in this situation voluntarily, but now that the game was afoot, I felt – and so did Amanda – that we should play this game to win. Our weapons were modern, but our instincts were basic and primitive.

183

Amanda and I were already moving for cover, me behind the bricks of the old fireplace, and she behind the garbage dumpster. Our gun-hands were ready to draw, but we were not going to be the first to show steel.

Before we got to cover, the starting flag flew. The two drug dealers in the argument at the end of the vacant lots did not realize the situation all around them, and one of them suddenly decided to dispose of the chubby man with the complaint.

The tall, skinny drug dealer produced from his jacket a silver revolver. The chubby man reached into the rear of his trousers, but he died with his hand in his pants. The air echoed with the sharp distinctive crack of two .357 magnum cartridges. The chubby man crumpled to the ground and rolled over into his own blood. His business was concluded.

All around the street, guns snapped out of holsters. Of course Amanda and I drew our pistols as well. Across the way, the three gang members at the projects produced two semi-automatic handguns and a 30-round mini-carbine. The three individuals waiting in the car exited their doors with guns ready. The driver and the female passenger had semi-autos, and the male passenger had a long-barreled .44 magnum revolver. The only ones who hadn't drawn a gun now were the dead man and the second of the two drug dealers. This fellow's reaction was slow, but in another moment he, too, drew a little mini semi-automatic.

After those first shots, there was a pause as we all got our guns out and prepared for further action. There was a moment in which it was still possible that the death toll could stop at just one. A gunfight here made no sense. Everyone out in the open, most of us heavily armed – The odds were in favor of death instead of life.

And yet, with emotions running high, with fingers on triggers, it was the more natural course that the shooting would continue, that death would take a quick and large harvest here. I thought once again about my partner Amanda, and my fear she would be hurt.

It was the driver of the car who made the fateful move to continue the gunfight. He let go a spray of pistol fire in the direction of the two drug dealers. He was shooting across a long distance and, like, most criminals, he was not a very good shot. He missed the two men standing, but he managed to pump two more bullets into the lifeless body of his friend as it lay on the ground. The corpse jerked horribly from the impact of the bullets planting themselves within it. A spurt of blood from the body sprayed one of the drug dealers.

In reaction to these shots, the gang across the street by the projects started shooting too. The guy with the mini-carbine hosed his bullets at the threesome who had come out of the car. He was another typical hoodlum with a high-capacity weapon; he didn't hit his targets, either. He did manage to puncture the radiator on his enemies' car, and he completely shattered the windshield on my Mercury and put some other bullet holes into my car's hood and roof. Glass was flying everywhere. "Goddamn it," I said. Even in a deadly gunfight, a guy still manages to notice his car being ruined.

One of the three gang members by the project stairway began firing at Amanda and me. It is one of the most remarkable sensations a human being can ever have, to have a bullet whizzing past you from the gun of someone trying to kill you. The young thug firing the gun had little sense of how to sight or aim a pistol, and so his bullets missed wildly, though a couple rang out on the garbage dumpster that was partly shielding Amanda.

The man who was shooting at us began to crouch behind a metal garbage can. I knew that the bullets in my gun could penetrate the metal, but also that the bullets might be deflected in their course and not reach the vital parts of this man behind the barrier. So I fired five shots into the garbage can at various points around a small circle. I would learn later I shot him in his weak arm; he was not yet put down.

The man I had been shooting at stood up, gun in hand, and ready to shoot some more at me in revenge for his wound. I heard Amanda's pistol fire immediately. Her first bullet struck the man's forehead right at the hairline. The scalp blew right off his head, and parts of his brain splattered his buddies.

Far to our left there still stood the two drug dealers, almost out in the open, and now firing across our front at the group outside the car. The man with the silver revolver who started the mess now made a second kill, but it was, tragically, not one of the other group of bad guys.

His last bullet flew past his assailants and struck an elderly grandmother of 63, wearing a pretty dress and hat and on her way to church. The poor woman spun full around from the impact of the bullet; she let go of her pink purse and it flew into the street.

In the slow-motion sensations of the gun battle, her short dying body seemed to spin almost forever, until she fell on her face in the gutter, her Sunday finery soiled with blood and grime. She bled to death in seconds, her dear grandchildren never to again experience her kind indulgence. It was just about the most awful thing I've seen in my life, to see an elderly woman die like that on her way to church.

The man who killed her did not live to learn his victim's name. Within seconds after shooting the old woman, he himself died, shot almost in the same moment both by Amanda and one of the people from the car.

I was still shooting my pistol across the street at the two remaining members of the gang by the projects, now taking cover behind a row of garbage receptacles. I couldn't be sure if I had yet hit one of them. One hand remained extended around a garbage can, blindly firing back in our direction.

Then the ears of everyone on the street were stunned to near bursting because one of the men from the car had begun firing his .44 magnum with full power buffalo-stopping ammo.

The .44 magnum had been aimed at *me*, and it blew away a large chunk of the brickwork on Uriah Jenkins' old fireplace. The .44 magnum is a good defense handgun against a bear or an angry moose, but it is a silly gun for an inexperienced criminal in a streetfight. The shock and recoil of the powerful .44 cartridge forced the man's gunhand straight up into the air. His big silver revolver pointed up at the clouds.

With the last two shots in my pistol I fired at him. The second shot struck him right in the armpit, and his still partly-loaded gun went flying as he fell to the pavement.

My gun was empty. I dumped the vacant cartridge chute, grabbed a second magazine from my belt, and loaded my pistol again. It was a very fast magazine-change, but it seemed horribly slow. The woman from the car had watched her friend with the .44 magnum get shot, and then in hatred she turned her pistol on me as I was loading up.

Amanda Poe's gun fired at her and missed because of the long distance. The woman sprayed her pistol at both of us; her desire to kill was fully unleashed. My gun now cocked and ready, I fired three shots at her, two of which entered her left breast. Blood spurted onto her peach-colored blouse as she fell to the ground, dead.

Amanda was now reloading. And then, for a few seconds of hell, all of the other three sides were firing at us. The drug dealer with the mini-gun, the men behind the garbage cans, the driver of the car and his buddy who had been shot in the armpit. The wounded guy who had lost his .44 had picked up the pistol of his dead girlfriend and was firing back at us with his weak hand.

For a moment I saw a house standing around me instead of a vacant lot. A fire blazed tall in the fireplace, and standing there was the long-dead Uriah Jenkins in his 19th-century clothes. I shouted a wordless yell, and my eyes came back to the modern reality of several people trying to kill me. Later, Amanda would tell me she saw the same thing.

Amanda and I fought back against our foes with a barrage of nearly two dozen rounds of ammunition. We emptied both our guns in three directions, Amanda taking on the guy with the mini-gun, me taking the two guys by the car, and both of us hitting the gang by the garbage cans.

I nailed the driver of the car who was shooting from behind his car door. My bullet went through the door and blew apart the man's groin; he fell to the street and bled to death. His partner, Mr. Magnum, used his last ammo to nail the second drug dealer at the end of the row, and so the guy with the mini-gun died with his face lying in the grass next to the chubby man who had been the first to die.

Amanda and I reloaded once more, Amanda starting first and then me, both of us finishing the same instant. I remember that moment in which the fresh (and final) spare magazines of our two pistols both clicked into place, and the hot slides of our guns slid forward to chamber the rounds within in the same second. With that syncopated loading of our pistols, I knew in that instant that we would win, and come out of this bloodbath just fine.

Amanda got a bead on the man with the wounded armpit and she shot him in his other arm. The bone shattered from the impact; that arm was amputated a few hours later, and the other arm would never fully recover. Although shot twice, that villain would live, one arm gone and other nearly useless.

Amanda and I now focused our guns on the one remaining target area, across the street at the garbage cans and the two men who might still be a threat behind them. A gun again emerged from the side of one of the cans and fired. Both Amanda and I pumped several bullets that way, and the garbage can spun away into the street as the hand shooting at us dropped its gun. The space left by the tossed trash can now showed two motionless bodies laying on the ground, not far from where their companion with the carbine lay dead.

Sirens could be heard in the distance. The cops were coming. Amanda and I kept our guns ready and pointed, the remainder of our ammo in reserve, but the gunfight was now over. The two men behind the garbage cans had both been critically shot; one of them would live, and one would die.

When the cops came they could barely believe it – even the ones who worked this neighborhood and had seen many a corpse on the ground, were flabbergasted. It was the wildest gunfight anybody could remember.

As the cavalry arrived I looked over at Amanda, her hot gun held firmly in her paw, her fingers darkened with the black mist of fired gunpowder. She looked majestic, proud and glorious.

It was now the second time that Amanda and I had stood side by side with guns drawn in a deadly situation. I didn't yet know if Amanda and I would ever or could ever be in love, but I did know that we had experienced something that brings people even closer together than romance.

The cops totalled up the scene after the ambulances took control of the wounded. Ten people had been discharging weapons, and about a hundred and forty rounds had been fired. Seven people were dead, including one very innocent bystander; one more was dying; and two were very seriously wounded. Of all the shooters, only Amanda and myself were all right.

As the cops drove Amanda and me downtown for the second post-shooting visit to police headquarters in as many months, I realized that the sweetest kind of prayer is the one where you say: Thanks a lot, God, for saving my ass. And I also told Him ditto, for keeping safe as well the pretty behind of my wonderful and mystical friend Amanda Poe.

The Colonel and the Tree

Almost as unnerving as the gunfight was the bureaucratic aftermath. Unlike the previous shooting in which I was involved, the heap of bodies that we left on 19th Street was a mess that seemed like it would never go away: Ten people shot, eight of them dead, including an innocent grandmother. I had now been in two deadly gun battles in less than a month. Naturally, the cops had some questions. What the hell was I doing in that neighborhood anyway?

As Amanda and I rode together to the police station, we both understood the need to keep secret the real reason for our visit to that vacant lot. It would be important to our employer Dabney Horton that we not disclose that we were working for him. More importantly, if we tipped off the police that the site was related to the serial murders, they would leak it to reporters and perhaps destroy our route to catching the murderer. We didn't want the killer reading in the newspapers about our research.

While we were riding together in the squad car, we got our stories into alignment. "What an awful experience," said Amanda, "Considering the real reason we went to that street." I knew that Amanda was actually asking me to state a reasonable story so she could play along. Two Richmond police officers were in the front seat of the car listening to us, so we had to be careful.

"Yeah," I replied, "You'd think Sunday morning would be a good time to look at some old townhouse sites for building and renovation, even in a bad neighborhood like that one. I don't think we're gonna want to buy any lots or do any building in that neighborhood, no matter how cheaply we can buy the property. It's just too damn dangerous."

Amanda looked at me crossly. I sounded a little phony, but the real-estate-investment story was the best fib I could think of at the moment as to why we were standing in the middle of a drug dealer zone when a gunfight started. Now that I'd said it, Amanda and I needed to stick to the story and pretend we were forming a real estate partnership to do some building in the ghetto. A pretty laughable idea, considering I didn't even pay my bills on time.

The cops in the front of the car cracked a joke about some people in the street and began to laugh, and I then I heard another voice laughing. The other voice was loud and cavernous, a deep male voice which overwhelmed the voices of the two cops and all other sounds. I looked at Amanda and I knew she could hear the strange laughter, too.

The laughter grew louder and louder until it was almost shrieking. It was a voice from the grave. The squad car seemed to disappear from around us, and all we saw was the face and form of Uriah Jenkins, laughing and howling with devilish joy. He had been there during the entire gunfight. Most of those who died in the gun battle were now with him.

Uriah was laughing at the violent deaths he helped inspire, laughing at a world that continued his legacy of evil, and laughing at the two detectives who almost died in tracking that legacy.

I felt Amanda's hand take hold of mine, and then the ghostly vision faded away. We were once again sitting quietly in the squad car, about to arrive at police headquarters. Amanda looked pale and fearful; this last vision of Uriah had upset her greatly, much more than it had upset me. It seemed to upset her even more than the gunfight, even more than the fact she had just helped to shoot and kill several human beings.

"Oh, God," said Amanda, wearily. "I wonder if we'll get through this."

"Yeah," I said, confident although I didn't know why. "We'll get through it." I put my hand on her side. "You're wonderful, Amanda," I said.

She smiled tentatively. "Thanks," she replied, in almost a whisper.

* * *

Down at the police station it was madness. Reporters, detectives, phones ringing and papers flying. Questions, questions and more questions. They didn't believe our story about being there to look for locations for possible real estate development, and so they pounded us with interrogations in separate rooms.

We were at the police station all afternoon, and from deep inside the investigation area we could hear the news reporters all clamoring in the hallway. Then, suddenly, Amanda and I were left alone, and escorted to a VIP reception room. There was one person waiting for us there – Jeffrey Mortimer, private secretary to Dabney Horton. The cops left us alone.

"Did you two do anything to start this gunfight?" he asked.

I held up my right hand. "No, sir!" I said.

"Neither of you shot the old lady, I take it?"

"That's right," said Amanda.

"Everything you two did in that Wild-West gun battle on the streets of Richmond was absolutely necessary?"

We both nodded.

"Well, Ms. Poe and Mr. Allan, I am glad that Mr. Horton is in good health, because he was liable to have had a heart attack this afternoon when he heard that special news bulletin about you two shooting up the projects. Were you two investigating that certain matter in which you have been retained, or was this some private lark?"

"It was a key part of the investigation," said Amanda. "I think we're close. We hoped to meet with Dabney soon." Amanda was of course fibbing, because we actually intended to avoid Horton until we pinned down everything about Uriah Jenkins.

Mortimer asked us if we had "Anything concrete to go on – Anything to be passed on to Mr. Horton?"

I stayed quiet. Amanda replied for us. "No," she said, "But we do have a trail."

"You understand the importance of your promise to confide in Mr. Horton before going to the police?"

"That's unconditionally guaranteed," I said.

"Well, all right, you two. We're all quite shocked at Mr. Horton's, but you will be pleased to know that Mr. Horton has undertaken certain efforts on your behalf.

"We've been in touch with the Richmond police commissioner, the Commonwealth's attorney, the state police and the newspapers. Things will be kept as low profile as possible under the circumstances. There will be no more questions about why you were at that location, and assuming the bystander was not killed by your bullets, there will be no charges filed regarding you two despite all the bodies.

"You still must cooperate with the authorities and answer all questions about what happened, excepting anything regarding the matter in which Mr. Horton has retained you. As it is, you are the principal witnesses to the tragic murder of that senior citizen. This is important to the community. Did you see who killed her?"

"Yes. He's dead," I replied.

"I see," said Mortimer. "Well, I remain at your service at any time on behalf of Mr. Horton. My regrets you've had such a terrible experience. Please *try* to stay out of trouble, for Mr. Horton's sake if not your own. Do you need any more money, or any other form of assistance? Legal advice, if needed, will of course be provided."

After Mortimer left, the cops returned to talk to us with a whole new attitude, much more deferential and positive. Even so, the questions continued for several more hours that day, and for several days afterwards as well. Amanda and I were forced to relive and repeat every moment of that gunfight, over and over again.

Somewhat unfortunately, two of the bad guys had survived the battle. They were shot and injured badly, but would recover enough to stand trial. The prosecutors regretted not having the man who shot the elderly woman still alive, because he would have been a good candidate for death by lethal injection.

The two surviving criminals would get long prison terms, and Amanda and I would later be called to testify in endless legal proceedings. The legal aftermath of this gunfight, we well knew, might follow Amanda and me for five years or more.

In the shorter term, the police interrogations tied us up for several days, and hindered us from going further in our murder investigation. We were not free of the bullshit until Thursday.

The entire week after the big gun battle, I had wild dreams when I slept. I dreamed of the gunfight, and also of the Old Mansion and Uriah Jenkins. Every night in my sleep I saw again that moment in the gunfight when I shot the bad young woman who had been part of the gang in the car.

I had every right to kill that woman, given the fact that she'd been shooting in our direction and intending to kill me in particular. But it was hard for me to get used to the idea that I had shot and killed a woman. This woman was a seedy character with a long criminal history. But in my old-fashioned view of things, I guess I put women on a pedestal. I assume they're basically sugar and spice and other things nice. But women can be felonious criminals, too.

After a while, I realized what *really* upset me about having shot a woman. I had killed a young woman, a young woman whom I might have found attractive if I hadn't seen her with a malicious scowl on her face firing a loaded gun at me. The fact that I had killed her made me feel as if I was perhaps just a tiny bit like Uriah Jenkins, or like the modern serial killer for whom we were looking. These men killed innocent young women for pleasure; although I had shot a criminally murderous young woman out of necessity, even so, I felt dirty about it.

The shoot-out by the housing projects bothered me afterwards a lot more than I'd been troubled by shooting those two hoods on Franklin Street. This was puzzling, because in both cases, everything I'd done was ethical and proper and legal.

But then I realized what was different. The second shooting incident was pervaded by the spirit of Uriah Jenkins, by the ghost of this long-dead murderous pervert. *He* had *wanted* that gunfight; *he* had inspired all those criminal fools to start pulling those triggers. Uriah knew that Amanda and I were looking for his ghost, and his spirit enjoyed setting us up in the middle of that deadly situation.

I would not have peace in my life until I solved the mystery of Uriah Jenkins. If I didn't find him out first and clear up the mystery about him, his evil spirit would find a way to kill *me*, and then I, too, would be a ghost.

Talking to Amanda over dinner on Thursday, the week of police grilling now behind us, I found that she felt the same way, too. She also felt that her life was in danger of being snuffed out under the evil influence of Uriah Jenkins.

I wished there was a way for me to ask Amanda to sleep with me that night, not for sex, but for the comfort, so that we could face our bad dreams together. But any way of posing the question seemed crude and so I avoided it.

So, after dinner, we went to our separate houses to bed, and resolved to continue our pursuit of Uriah Jenkins the next morning. I was lucky, however, to see Amanda in my dreams. In the dream, she kissed me. In the morning I wondered if she had had the same dream, but I didn't ask her.

* * *

Friday morning found Amanda and me once again on the road, back to Louisa county and the neighborhood of Uriah Jenkins' old plantation. My car had partially recovered from the damage it sustained during the big 19th Street gunfight. There was new window glass and some mechanical repairs, but there were still bullet holes in the sheet metal. It reminded me of "Bonnie & Clyde's death car" that I once saw on display somewhere.

Amanda said she couldn't quite explain why we were going back out to Louisa, but that she knew it was the best place to continue our quest to find out what really happened to Uriah Jenkins when he disappeared in 1859. I trusted Amanda's instincts enough to go along with her, but I found myself angry with her as we drove along Virginia's country roads to our destination.

Why was I mad at Amanda? I didn't say anything to her about how I felt. I looked deep within myself for the reasons. And then I knew why I was mad. It was my male ego.

Amanda was a lovely and wonderful woman who had abilities I did not have, who could do things that I couldn't do. I couldn't even pretend to myself that I was the totally self-sufficient male in charge of the whole situation.

I realized it was time to grow up, and face the fact I could be out-done by a woman in at least *some* ways. I made a mental resolution to be more comfortable with Amanda leading and me following.

I looked over at Amanda across the armrest of my car, and she was smiling a wicked smile at me. "Are you still mad?" she asked. Damn it, how could she know what I was thinking! Did she know my fantasies about her as well?

I wasn't mad anymore, but I was unnerved. Not only did I have to watch what I said around Amanda, I even had to watch what I was *thinking*.

* * *

For a while after we got to Louisa county, we just drove around. We drove through town, past the police station and the morgue. We drove past the Baptist church where we had talked to the pastor, past the simple homes of the descendants of Horton family slaves, past the places on the back roads where the bodies of the murdered women had been discovered, and past the place where we had parked my car the night we spent at the Old Mansion.

I didn't know what we were looking for, but Amanda seemed to have a purpose in our wanderings. "Turn this way," she would say, or "Why don't we go down here?" Up and down the roads we drove. To me it was all just a bunch of country scenery, but I could see the little wheels turning in Amanda's exotic mind. She was feeling things, seeing things in another dimension. Through the late morning and early afternoon, she said she felt we were getting somewhere, somehow getting closer to solving the mystery of Uriah Jenkins' ghost. Finally, she exclaimed: "Stop!"

We were on a tiny road, just a couple of miles from the spooky Old Mansion where Uriah Jenkins' ghost still held sway. Just off the road, in a clearing between some trees, was a small decrepit little house with a broken-down porch. I had a strange feeling in my heart – compassion and sadness, combined with dread. Amanda's face was lit up like a lamp.

The air today was beautifully scented with Virginia's native flora. We parked at the edge of the roadway behind a ten-year-old Plymouth, and I silently followed Amanda on the twig-strewn pathway toward the little shack. A middle-aged woman emerged to greet us. She was an African-American woman with a face that looked slightly familiar, though I knew I had not met her before.

"I'm Amanda," said my partner, in a tone that suggested the woman was expecting her, "And this is David."

"I have known," said the woman slowly, and with emphasis, "I have known all my life that someone like you would come. My mother, my grandmother, and my great-grandmother all said there would be a day, a day when the truth would be known. My name is Ida Brown, and you're here to ask me about the last Jenkins, aren't you?"

I started to speak but Amanda touched my arm, indicating to me to keep quiet. We stood there silently for a second as Ida looked at us. The wind blew gently and evocatively through the ancient Virginia woods.

Then Ida spoke again. "It's a simple message I give you, a message the womenfolk in my family have passed on for seven generations. I've never told my children. Deep down I knew that I would be the one to help tell this thing to the world, and so I wanted to give my children a chance never to have a nightmare about the Jenkins secret. They'll never know, bless them, about what really happened to my long ago mama. You are the ones who are here to find the truth, isn't that so?"

"That's right, we are," I answered. Amanda nodded and touched Ida gently.

"What I was told by my mama to tell you, is this: 'Look for the big tree by the little river.' That's all. 'The big tree by the little river.' I won't say nothin' more." With that, Ida Brown began to cry.

Amanda kissed her on the cheek. "Yes, Ms. Brown, you've done what your family always wanted you to do. I hope you live long and live in peace, and that you never have a bad dream again."

I bowed respectfully, and Ms. Brown then took my hand in hers and caressed it. She hugged Amanda, and then I saw Amanda's movements directing us to leave. "Take good care, Ms. Brown!" said Amanda.

"I'll pray for you!" she said, still crying but happy. "I'll pray for both of you!" She waved to us, we waved back at her as we got into my car.

She waited outside her house to watch us leave. I carefully backed onto the little dirt road, and I waited till we had driven out of sight before I spoke. "What happened there?" I asked Amanda.

Amanda was crying a little herself. "Hold on a second," she said, while she wiped away her sniffles. "David, Ida Brown is a direct descendant of one of the women whom Uriah

Jenkins tortured and murdered in the 1850s. Did she look familiar to you?" – I nodded – "Well, you saw her ancestor at the Old Mansion. She was one of the victims in the torture room. That was who Ida meant by 'long ago mama'."

Amanda continued to explain. "That young slave whom Uriah Jenkins tortured to death, she left a little baby that was cared for by other slaves. Ida Brown is a descendant. Part of the slave community knew or found out not only how terribly some of their group had died, but also about what happened to Uriah.

"Some one of these ex-slaves was gifted as well with sight into a future day when the truth would come out. This gift was passed on to Ida Brown, who knew it was a mission of her life to pass on the clue to the strangers, namely *us*, who would ask about it.

"So it turns out, David, that you and I are a predestined part of history. Long ago it was settled that you and I would one day come to Ida Brown's house, and learn the clue to finally solving the Uriah Jenkins mystery."

I pondered for a moment the increasingly mystical view of the world that I was getting from being around Amanda. Then I asked her, "Should we have questioned the woman any more?"

"No," said Amanda. "We'll find out everything else we need to know. It was a painful family memory for the Browns all these years, and Ida wanted to finally close the book on the story of the slaves who were raped and murdered so long ago. I think we should leave her in peace."

"'Big tree by the little river'," I repeated. "Any idea where that is?"

"There aren't that many rivers in Louisa county," answered Amanda. "I'm sure we'll find it soon."

* * *

In truth, it wasn't long before we did find the right river, an ancient tributary of the larger South Anna River that still bore its old Native American name: The Pataquoy, a small stream that coursed amid swampy and rocky shores, a river whose views and vistas were little touched by time.

As we drove over the Pataquoy across a bridge, Amanda knew immediately it was the river we wanted to find. "The exact spot is not far," she said, with commanding intuition. "It's just up the stream. That's where we need to go."

Just south of the bridge I spotted an old house by the water, with several canoes and other boats lying next to the pier in back of it. I guessed the owner probably rented the boats in the summer, but it was not summer yet.

Country people can be very friendly to a polite stranger, and so we made the effort to knock on the door and meet the family who owned the house and the boats. We spent a half hour there visiting, and at the end of that time, with the offering of a proper amount of cash, the best of the boats was in our hands. We stowed our camping gear in it, and Amanda and I went up river.

It was early evening as we began to proceed slowly toward where we hoped to learn the final fate of Uriah Jenkins when he was alive in the previous century. It was an absolutely beautiful Virginia day, and Amanda and I were alone on the water. Very few houses were visible

214

from the stream; the shore alternated between heavy woods, rocky ledges, or swamp, much as the Native Americans must have seen it before the coming of the white man.

I looked at Amanda in the late afternoon sun, and she was beautiful indeed. It was a sweet moment, being alone with her on such a nice day, amid the soothing wonders of nature. I regretted we were on such a dark and important mission. I wished we had no such agenda, and were only there on the river to enjoy the world and life and one another.

Geographically, we were not too far from the Old Mansion where we'd seen Jenkins' ghost. We weren't more than six miles distant, and the river was curving in a line that kept it close to the plantation grounds.

About three miles up from the bridge we both saw it: An ancient oak, several hundred years old, just in from the riverbank. I felt chilled right down to my bones. There was also a place to pull in to shore. Without either of us saying a word, we both knew this was the place to stop. In a matter of hours we would know the fate of Uriah Jenkins.

* * *

We got our gear off the boat and looked around. There were no man-made artifacts visible. It all seemed innocent enough, except for a very profound feeling that Amanda and I both shared about this location. "I take it we're spending the night?" I asked. Amanda nodded. Then I said, "Any idea what we can learn from this place?"

"I'm sure we'll know by morning," she answered. We both laughed, a little nervously.

It was almost sunset. We gathered wood for our campfire, set up our tent, had some dinner, and we cuddled close as the sun set on the Pataquoy. I put my arm around her and she put her head on my shoulder. This felt good.

For a while after dark, we talked about this and that, about not very important things, such as projects we wanted to undertake after this case was over. Finally, it seemed time to go to sleep under the stars.

Amanda surprised me by kissing me. "See you in my dreams," she said, in a way that made me know she meant it. As usual in a new setting, I dropped off to sleep with my hand on my holstered pistol.

* * *

When I awoke, it was the middle of the night and I was staring into the campfire. It was very cold despite the fire, which had strangely grown much larger. I guessed that Amanda must have thrown on more firewood while I was sleeping.

Suddenly I realized that I was not lying down, I was standing! My first instinct with this disorientation was to feel for my gun, and it was right there tight against my side. I looked around and Amanda was standing next to me, her eyes alive and nearly wild. She smiled at me with a knowing look of supernatural intensity.

Then I noticed as well that we were not alone. Several other people, seven in all, were there nearby, along with a number of horses. Three of them wore military uniforms of a kind I did not recognize. One of them had a large plume in his hat, topping off the outfit of a high-ranking officer in some army of long ago. The other men wore costume-like dress clothes of a style from the last century. One of the men was facing away from us, with his hands tied behind his back.

A civilian among the group addressed the man with the plume in his hat, calling him "Colonel Horton." But he was not the Dabney Horton I knew.

The group of strangers turned around the man whose hands were tied: He was Uriah Jenkins, and he looked *straight* at me and Amanda, his eyes burning with a combination of hate and fear. I felt a wave of horror break over me. Uriah Jenkins, now seemingly a living human being, stared at me and Amanda for an achingly long moment, as if he recognized us clearly!

I opened and closed my eyes twice. I could feel the cold night air biting my cheeks. I pinched my arm and felt the pain. I was completely awake and alive. I looked at Amanda and she nodded, answering my unspoken question.

This was on a completely different level from our previous visions and dreams and nightmares. Where we were now, and what we were seeing, was completely real. Somehow, under the influence of Amanda's great spiritual power, Amanda and I had gone *back* in time and space. We were now in Virginia in 1859! We were at the same spot on the Pataquoy River in Louisa County, but everything was different. The trees, the river, the stars: It was the way it was a hundred years before I was even born.

Aside from Uriah, the group did not seem to notice Amanda and myself. We were living in a moment of history, but unseen by its participants, except for the murderer and future evil ghost Uriah Jenkins.

"Colonel Horton," said one of the gentlemen, in a lovely, ancient, syrupy Virginia voice of a kind that is rarely heard anymore, "I'd like to ask once more if we are all certain there is no other way to resolve the issue of this man's crimes. We all know he needs to be hanged, but is it really the way of gentlemen not to do this through an open court of law and a public gallows?"

"Sir," replied the Colonel, "I honor the intention of your question. If times were not what they were, I would surely say that the ordinary course of law was the only proper manner to send this man to his grave.

"But," Colonel Horton continued, "I have weighed this matter in my mind and I have come to absolute certainty. We are on the verge of a terrible war with our brothers in the states of the North. I believe it is still possible for that war to be avoided, and I believe that as gentlemen we owe it to the women and children of the South to do what we can to avoid that war.

"My distant cousin Uriah Jenkins, whom we are about to hang from this tree, is a slave killer, a man who has raped and cut and killed Negro women, and also a gentle white woman, to serve his perverted and devilish pleasures.

"The newspapers in the North would seize on any public proceedings regarding his crimes, as an excuse for all-out war on the South. This true story of the plantation owner who rapes and mutilates his slaves, would become the battle-cry of the Northern war-mongers.

"If we do not accomplish the judgment and punishment of Uriah Jenkins in secret, many thousands of innocent people could die. Our way of life could be lost, and there might come a new America where gentlemen would lose many of their personal liberties to a tyrannical national government.

"Gentlemen, this hanging must be done here and now, so as to avoid or at least postpone a terrible civil war." The Colonel paused and looked around at everyone in the group. Uriah Jenkins glared at the men and muttered darkly. The men started to nod their agreement.

"I ask for your consent, from each one of you, to this hanging at this tree, and also your solemn promise not to tell anyone what happens here, and what we have together done to help save the South."

One by one, each in the party gave his approval to the deathly course of the night's proceedings. Then, Colonel Horton himself produced the rope from his saddlebag, the end already bound in a hangman's noose, and threw the rope around a stout branch of the large oak tree.

The group stood the cursing Uriah Jenkins underneath the rope and placed the noose around his neck. "Fuck you!" said Uriah. "Fuck and goddamn all of you!" His voice chilled me to the core. Amanda touched me, and I knew she felt as I did.

"Uriah Jenkins," said the Colonel, "You are guilty of the dishonorable crimes of raping, dismembering and murdering both Negro women and a gentlewoman, of violating your trust as an owner of slaves, and of bringing disgrace and the risk of bloody war upon your home country of Virginia. By our authority as militia of Virginia, and because of our duty to deal with your crimes in a manner that is most likely to save this Commonwealth, we are going to hang you from this tree by the neck until you die, and we will bury you here in a grave unmarked and unknown.

"Uriah Jenkins, do you have anything to say before you are hanged? Would you like time to make a prayer and confess your sins to God, lest you burn in hell forever?"

"Fuck you, *Colonel* Horton," said Uriah, "And fuck the rest of you cowardly bastards! I'll see you in hell. You prancing fools, you've never known what I've known, the pleasure of fucking a woman that you've stabbed, to fuck her while the blood still flows from the wounds you've given her. To fuck her while she screams, fuck her while she's dying, and fuck her again after she's dead. It's a glory better than God himself knows, a glory that I will take with me for all eternity. I've fucked women like none of you will ever fuck, you stinking, milquetoast *gentlemen.*

"Don't even have the courage to hang me in public, *do you,* you slimy worms? You're afraid to tell about my *glorious* fucking of my ladyfriends, my dead, bleeding ladyfriends, you bastards! I'm going to come *back* from the *grave* and kill some more ladyfriends, and fuck them right to *death,* how do you like *that,* Colonel Horton and you gentlemen? Fuck you all to *hell* right after me!"

Jenkins glared at the group with anger, hatred, and fear; and also some perverted sense of triumph. It was as if he actually was glad, in his dying hour, to have committed his horrible crimes, despite being hanged for them in the end.

The entire group was silent for a moment, everybody's soul weighted down with the profundity of what they were about to do. "Tighten the rope," said Colonel Horton. A horse was brought up, and Uriah Jenkins was lifted onto the horse's bare back. The rope's position was adjusted on the tree branch, and looped over the stout limb a second time. The other end of the rope was tied securely around the tree trunk.

Colonel Horton spoke a last time to Uriah Jenkins. "You will suffer for a number of minutes as you die by hanging, Uriah Jenkins. I hope that in those minutes you reflect on the suffering you have caused to others."

"It'll remind me of some of the *special* pleasures I've had," said Uriah, a relentless criminal pervert even in the final moments of his life. "Fucking cowardly bastards!" he shouted, his final words to his executioners. Uriah then himself fell silent, seemingly waiting for his own death-agony to begin.

I put my hand on my pistol, undid the safety strap, and clicked off the safety catch. My gun was ready to fire. I had always been a believer in law and not in vigilante justice. I had enough bullets to save Uriah from the lynching group, and my instincts as a cop were to try and stop the hanging and bring the whole group to a courthouse.

I was standing there along a riverbank in 1859, in a time and place a hundred and twenty-five years before the pistol in my hand was even invented. I felt sure, in that moment, that I *could*, if I wanted, change the course of history.

I looked at Amanda and she was looking at me with utter seriousness. She shook her head with grave authority, and I understood. It was not our role to intervene in history, even if supernatural powers had placed us in its midst. The hanging of Uriah Jenkins would proceed.

Colonel Horton slapped the horse's behind and the animal lunged forward, leaving Uriah Jenkins to dangle at the rope's end. I took a deep breath and gazed upon the disturbing sight of an execution in progress. Uriah's eyes bulged, the tongue came out of his mouth. He was a horrible figure there, a hanged but still living man in the moonlight. He made awful groaning sounds. His legs kicked wildly. I thought I could still see in Uriah's tormented face his obsession with sadistic murder, and I imagined that he was still mentally indulging the details of his crimes as he struggled for air and life.

There was a stench as Uriah lost control of his bowels. It was a very slow death. With Uriah still kicking and slowly strangling, one of the men said, "Let's dig his grave." Three of them began to dig while the other three, and myself and Amanda, watched Uriah Jenkins die.

It was an awful sight, seeing a human being slowly strangle at the end of a rope. But I kept in mind the memory of the women that Uriah had raped and murdered, women I had seen with my own eyes at the Old Mansion, and I could not feel any sorrow or regret for him. My final thought as I watched Uriah's hanging body grow dead and still, was that this hanging by a small mob of old Southern gentlemen did seem to serve the purpose of justice, despite its coarse brutality.

As Uriah's corpse swung gently now from the tree, Uriah's spirit now begun on its long journey of haunting the Virginia of the future, I looked over at Amanda. She continued to look at the hanged man with a deep and brooding gaze. I so hated for a woman to be seeing this. But I also knew that it was only *because* of Amanda that we were seeing this at all. Pain and death were topics very well known to her dark and mystical soul.

The grave was well-dug before Uriah Jenkins had been dead very long. The group stood a while observing his swaying body in the breeze. "We should be sure he is dead," said one of the men. The other men clearly felt the same need for assurance.

Colonel Horton drew his ancient revolver, cocked it, and fired directly into the heart of Uriah Jenkins' corpse. The body swung backwards with great force from the impact of the bullet. Blood flowed from the corpse's chest and bloodied his shirt. For a minute the corpse swung to and fro, and then gradually settled back to being still, just twisting slightly in the cold night breeze.

Shortly afterwards the Colonel used his sword to cut the body down. They tossed the body into the grave with the rope that had hanged him, and they covered him up. When they were all done, the men stood around the grave and collected their thoughts. Some of them were obviously saying silent prayers; whether for themselves or for the man they had hanged, I could not tell.

The Colonel said, "Let's get some sleep, gentlemen. You have all done your duty for Virginia." Leaving absolutely nothing at the site, the group put out the fire, got on their horses and rode away, taking one riderless steed with them.

As the horses receded into the distance, I felt my own eyes get drowsy. I thought I would close my eyes just for a second. But I saw no more of the moonlit woods of 1859. When I awoke it was dawn, and Amanda was lying on the good earth next to me. The sun was shining, the birds were chirping, and we emerged from the tent and saw the tree limb where the rope had suspended Uriah's body. The limb was thicker and longer, the tree was taller and wider, but we could still make out the exact spot where the rope was fastened, and the plot of brush where Uriah Jenkins' skeleton was buried.

What we had seen last night was awful, but what we had seen had given us knowledge and truth. We knew now what had happened to the owner of the Old Mansion. The mystery of the 19th century slave killer was a mystery no longer. It was now time to get back to chasing another killer of our own time, who was yet to receive *his* due portion of final justice.

The Family Honor

On Monday morning I picked up Amanda and we made our way to Dabney Horton's fancy office. Our purpose was to confront him with what we had learned about Uriah Jenkins.

Did Dabney know about the secret hanging organized in 1859 by his ancestor Colonel Horton, who would later become the hero of the Civil War? More importantly, would Dabney allow the story of the vigilante hanging to be publicized, and change the historical view of his ancestor?

While we were on our way to Dabney's office, Amanda once again explained to me why it was important that the truth about Uriah Jenkins be made known.

"Uriah's ghost has been haunting the Old Mansion, and haunting Virginia, because nobody knew the truth about how he'd died. His earthly destiny wasn't finished. When the truth about Uriah's life and death, about his murders and his lynching, when that story goes into the records of Virginia history, that's when his ghost will not bother this world again. And it'll be a snap to find our killer who murdered the three women, because Uriah's dead spirit will no longer be protecting him."

I still had a hard time understanding it. "Why," I asked, "Why won't Uriah still be involved with the murderer who's on our streets today? Won't they still be partners in crime?"

"No," said Amanda. "Uriah won't be interested anymore. The killer will be on his own. Everything that Uriah does, every time his ghost appears to someone, or he gives someone an evil idea, it's because he is drawing attention to himself. He's screaming in people's minds because he wants to tell his story. Because he can't tell the story directly, he involves people in horror and violence. Inspiring a chain of murders is a brutally effective way to get attention. Even that gunfight that caught us a week ago Sunday, that was Uriah's ghost starting trouble and making noise to announce himself."

"So at that empty lot where we had the big shoot-out, that's where the killer and the ghost of Uriah first met each other's minds?"

"I'm sure of that," said Amanda.

"Does that mean our killer is a drug dealer? That's the main reason anyone would visit that block."

"Or," suggested Amanda, "Maybe he's someone who lives nearby. Or maybe he's a real estate developer who was looking for a possible location for some new construction." We both smiled.

"For sure, though," Amanda continued, "We've *got* to get the Uriah Jenkins/Colonel Horton story out to scholars and the Civil War magazines and maybe even into the newspaper. The ghost has got to hear people talking about how he lived and died. That will keep the ghost out of our way, and let us pick up the trail of the rapist-murderer who's now stalking central Virginia."

"You know," I said, "I'm not sure Dabney Horton is going to *like* publicizing the fact that his ancestor led an antebellum lynch mob in defense of slavery and the South. It's not the usual image they present of the gentleman Colonel.

"When Colonel Horton hanged Uriah, you might say that he was being patriotic and trying to protect his mother-land of Virginia, but it's also true he was trying to cover up for the abuse of slaves that the whole institution of slavery had made possible. Not to mention the fact that Uriah Jenkins himself, one of the worst criminals in Virginia history, was a damned *relative* of Horton's, too."

"A *very* distant cousin," said Amanda, sticking up a bit for her blueblood friends the Hortons. "I don't think Dabney will have a problem with us publicizing the story. He'll be uncomfortable, but it's ancient history now, and there's been all sorts of Horton family scandals, at least one or two every generation.

"Dabney won't take the activities of some antebellum great-great-grandfather personally. Colonel Horton will still be the hero of

Petersburg, even if he did lynch a murderer once before the Civil War started.

"We've just got to convince Dabney to let us give out the story, so we can get ahead and find the killer of the three women. We've got to have Dabney on board, because nobody is going to publish anything like this about the Hortons without consulting with the Horton family first. The Hortons are so powerful, everyone would be afraid to step on their toes."

I didn't share Amanda's optimism about Dabney letting us share the story of the Uriah Jenkins hanging. My instinct was that the rich old coot would try to squash the whole thing and keep it quiet.

Amanda was Dabney's friend, but my trepidation turned out to be right on target.

* * *

When we first got to Dabney's office, he was very much the gracious host. He didn't talk business and he didn't mention the gunfight, or how he'd helped us avoid the legal consequences of that mess of a wild shoot-out.

Dabney offered us drinks, talked about the weather, and showed us some new paintings in his office. His beautiful new works of art were by Scarlett Samuels, a talented 19th century painter who was just beginning to get the recognition she deserved. Scarlett Samuels was a young woman in Richmond at the same time that Uriah Jenkins was walking its streets. I wondered if they had by chance ever seen one another. The paintings were magnificent romantic landscapes with young lovers pictured in them. I didn't know much about art, but I liked Dabney's new paintings a great deal.

As Dabney talked to us about his new art acquisitions, wearing his impeccable thousand-dollar suit and speaking in his wonderful old Richmond accent, I thought about how Dabney was the complete embodiment of the contemporary Virginia patriarch, the late-20th-century equivalent of an old plantation owner.

Finally we got down to some business. Dabney spoke about our recent shoot-out and its aftermath. "Sorry I couldn't get you out of those discussions at the police station sooner," he apologized. "I hate long meetings myself.

But with all that happened on the street, I'm sure you understand." We nodded. "You're a brave pair, you two," said Dabney, complimenting us. "Especially you, Amanda. I'm glad women can defend themselves, but it's the old gentleman in me to regret a lady would be in that kind of situation."

Amanda smiled. Now Dabney turned to the case for which we had been hired, our search for the triple murderer of young women.

"You two haven't been keeping me informed," Dabney complained, gently. "It's the least you could do, considering." Dabney grinned. "Why don't you bring me up to date and tell me what you've found so far?"

Amanda was blunt in her reply. "Dabney, it's what you feared. These murders are connected to the past, the past of your own family." Dabney's face grew cloudy and troubled. Obviously, he had some idea of what she was talking about.

* * *

"There was a murderer," said Amanda, "A murderer of young women, at large in Virginia in the 1850s." Dabney looked intently at us and said nothing, waiting for her to continue.

"The killer's name was Uriah Jenkins," said Amanda. "He was a distant cousin of your ancestor, Colonel Horton, the hero of the Civil War." Amanda nodded toward the portrait of the Colonel on Dabney's wall. Dabney remained impassive, and did not seem surprised by the information.

"Off the back roads in Louisa county," Amanda went on, "There is an old plantation house, still owned by you. Both the house and the grounds are neglected and abandoned. It is a place where, in the 1850s, a number of young women died in terrible agony, raped and stabbed to death and mutilated. One was a white woman, from a neighboring house, but most of the victims were slaves, most of them from Uriah Jenkins' own human 'property'."

Dabney still did not say a word.

"Uriah Jenkins came to Richmond sometimes on business, where he traded in slaves and other commerce of the day. He rented a townhouse, a townhouse on 19th Street. All that's left there today are some stones from the foundation and part of the old fireplace, but otherwise it's an empty lot. David and I almost got shot to death there a few days ago."

Dabney's eyes had grown wider. "I didn't know about the townhouse," he said.

"Sometime in 1859," continued Amanda, "A few local gentry of Virginia learned about these horrors, and they took action against Uriah Jenkins. Led by Colonel Horton, these men took an unusual step which they felt was in the best interests of Virginia. They decided to hush up both the murders and the identity of the killer.

"They felt that exposing the horrible nature of these slave-murders would fuel Northern anger and accelerate the destruction of the Union, and maybe start a civil war two years before Lincoln was even President. They were probably correct in thinking that an open trial of Jenkins might have accelerated or even ignited the War Between the States."

"That's right," said Dabney. "Ironically, though, I think the South would have won if the

War had started in 1859 instead of 1861. The North was not ready yet."

I was awestruck at the thought of how the hanging of one man might have changed the whole course of American history. Amanda went on with her story, some of which was clearly already known to Dabney.

"One night in 1859," she said, "In a small clearing off the Pataquoy River, Colonel Horton and a handful of his fellows brought Uriah Jenkins to a large oak tree with a high stout limb pointing toward the water. In that private place under the stars, they hanged Uriah Jenkins, and watched him die a slow death in the noose. They buried him a few yards away. They swore among themselves to keep the secret, and it never became public what happened to the slaves and the other woman who was murdered. The story was that they, like Uriah Jenkins himself, just 'disappeared'. But you knew a lot of this already, Dabney, didn't you?"

"Remarkable," said Dabney. "How does this relate to the killer of three Richmond women in these recent weeks? I grant you the bodies have been left near the Old Mansion.

But how can events nearly a century and a half ago, have anything to do with crimes in the present?" His tone was not quite skeptical, as if he suspected there was a connection, but was still trying to deny his own hunches.

Amanda leaned forward in her chair. "It's a consequence of the secret nature of the hanging of Uriah Jenkins. Because the truth never came out, Uriah's ghost still stalks the earth. His spirit haunts the Old Mansion, and it still haunts where we had the shoot-out last week. His ghost has entwined itself with the mind and soul of some twisted person who has now become Virginia's Jack the Ripper."

"What are you saying?" asked Dabney, getting testy now. "Are you implying that this killer is to be excused because he's under the influence of a ghost? Is the devil making him do what he's doing?"

"No," said Amanda. "The killer is guilty of the murders he committed this year, just like Uriah was guilty of those murders in the last century. The modern killer needs to be punished for his crimes, too. But his punishment needs to come openly, and it's also time for the story of Uriah Jenkins to come out.

"Dabney, it's the only way. Only by finally telling the truth about the secret hanging, about Colonel Horton and his cousin Uriah, can we have the full means to track down this killer."

Everyone was quiet a moment. Dabney looked actually nervous. "How did you find out all this?" he asked.

"Trade secret," said Amanda. "You know I've got some unusual techniques."

"It's our job to find things out. We're detectives," I said, somewhat stupidly. Dabney glared at me.

"You talked about that secret hanging like you were there," Dabney noted. He didn't realize how accurate his statement was. "I can't imagine how you could have found that out. And I suppose there's no harm in me talking about it with you now."

Dabney sat back in his chair. "A few of the men in my family have always known about Colonel Horton and the hanging of the slave killer. It's a family secret, partly unpleasant, but also a matter of family pride and honor.

242

Colonel Horton tried to save the Old South, and perhaps he did indeed prevent the Civil War from starting two years earlier.

"When I was twenty-seven years old, my father took me to that spot on the Pataquoy River, and he showed me Uriah Jenkins' grave and the tree where they hanged him. I did not understand the real meaning of the incident when I was that young, but since then I've come to appreciate the delicacy and importance of the issues involved, even more so now that I'm head of the Horton family and one of the leading citizens of Virginia.

"Yes, the story of that bit of classic justice is a part of my family's heritage. It's a very private part, however, and I expect it to remain that way."

I looked over at Amanda. Regrettably, I had been right. I just *knew* that Dabney would have a problem with going public with what we had discovered.

Dabney continued. "I don't have many more details about it than you do, but if it will help, I'll be glad to share them in confidence."

243

"What else do you know?" asked Amanda.

"Well, I do know that the story of the murders was revealed by a male slave named Jonathan who had heard the screams of the victims in Uriah's mansion, and who spied on Uriah when one of the bodies was being buried.

"Jonathan first took the story of the killings to a neighboring plantation, where he dared to tell the tale to a man who was Colonel Horton's brother-in-law. The first response was unfortunate. They took the slave to be a malicious liar, and he was given several whippings, more than the legal limit in lashes, which nearly killed him.

"Colonel Horton was present at one of those whippings, and I understood it nearly broke his heart to see the poor slave whipped and whipped again, with his back scarred and bleeding from previous punishments. Apparently, the man's composure and refusal to change his story convinced the Colonel to investigate further. The Colonel hired a man to spy on Uriah, and Uriah was caught red-handed chaining another slave to his dungeon wall.

"They searched the area for graves and found where the victims were buried, all of them having been horribly stabbed and mutilated. They found the bodies of all the slaves, and also the corpse of the woman from the Wallenford family who had been reported as missing.

"Colonel Horton accepted the responsibility for the secret hanging in order to, as he saw it, save Virginia from war and destruction. The day after the hanging, he paid a great sum of money to buy the brave slave Jonathan from his owner. Colonel Horton personally apologized to him, and nursed his wounds himself. When Jonathan was recovered, Colonel Horton gave him his freedom and a sack of gold coins. I don't know what happened to that brave black man, but he was the hero of the affair. That's really all I know.

"In my family," Dabney concluded, "Those destined for leadership are told the story of the Colonel and Uriah Jenkins underneath the hanging tree, as a means of instruction in the family honor, and the sometimes unpleasant and serious nature of duty to society. It is a tale we do *not* share with the world."

Dabney's last sentence seemed definitive as far as his position on disclosure was concerned, but Amanda leapt to press her point.

"Dabney," she said, "We've *got* to tell this story publicly. We've got to tell scholars, journals, Civil War magazines, maybe even the press. The ghost of Uriah Jenkins is haunting us today because his crimes and punishments were kept secret. The only reason he's inspiring and protecting the killer on our streets is to draw attention to himself. We need the truth to come out, or otherwise we may not be able to catch our killer."

"No, that's impossible," replied Dabney. "And I can't believe that your investigation would be limited by my continuing to keep a family secret more than a century old."

Amanda started to sound shrill and angry. "When you hired us to do this investigation, you *knew* from the way the victims were mutilated, and from where the bodies were being dumped, you *knew* this had something to do with Uriah

Jenkins, you knew, didn't you, didn't you, Dabney?"

Dabney Horton remained calm. "There was a certain similarity, that's all. And as I told you, I do feel a responsibility for that county where my family has long had old estates, and where many citizens are descended from my family's slaves."

"Dabney, we have to tell this story, and we're *going* to tell it!" Amanda threatened.

"Out of the question. End of discussion," said Dabney, with some confidence.

"Dabney, if we don't reveal the Uriah Jenkins story," said Amanda, "Another innocent young woman could die horribly, and that'd be on your conscience."

"That's *ridiculous*," said Dabney, now angry. "You two better get back to work, or perhaps you'd like to find another project."

Amanda stared at him for a moment and calmed herself. Then she said, "What if we have a television crew on the Pataquoy River while we dig up Uriah Jenkins' bones? They'll have a special program on the secret execution that helped postpone the Civil War!"

Dabney's eyes glowed with fire, and Amanda's dark eyes glared back with a flame equally intense. For several seconds nobody said anything.

Then Dabney spoke, sure of himself and in control. "Before you leave this building," he promised, "A crew will be on its way to that site. Those remains will be exhumed and reinterred where you can't find them. No one will publish your story, no one will believe you, and if you try to fight me, I will disassociate myself from you and destroy you."

There was a long pause while we pondered being threatened by one of Virginia's most powerful men. We knew we had lost this battle – Dabney would move the skeleton of the hanged Jenkins, and his friends who owned the newspapers and television stations and ran the universities would see that nothing was publicized no matter how hard we tried. We also knew that, just as easily as he had gotten us out of trouble with the law, he could swiftly take a brutal revenge on us if he so wished.

Dabney softened his victory with an imperial flourish. "Right now," he said, "I'd like

248

you two to continue working on the case." He reached into a drawer. "Here's your next month's pay and expenses," and handed us each an envelope containing $5000 in cash.

Weaklings that we were, there was no other choice but to take the money and keep trying to catch the killer somehow, even if we couldn't do what Amanda said we needed to do by way of exposing some of the Horton family dirty linen.

"Now please leave immediately," said Dabney. "And don't forget your promise. Turn up anything concrete about the murderer and you call me *first* – I mean before the police, or any other authority or anyone else whomsoever. I'm trusting your word as a gentleman." He looked me straight in the eye.

"Yeah," I said, "We'll call you first." I didn't want to promise Dabney anything, but I had promised the same thing before to him, and the five thousand bucks in my hand confirmed my sense of obligation.

"Good day," he said. I nodded. Amanda did not say a word. She turned on her heel and stormed out the door, full of anger and energy and beauty.

A Tale of Edgar Allan Poe

The meeting with Dabney perturbed Amanda far worse than any of our other experiences together. Neither the frights of the Old Mansion, nor Uriah's ghost, nor even the deadly rain of bullets in our big gunfight, had unsettled Amanda as much as Dabney Horton's insistence on keeping his family secret.

Amanda was shocked and overwhelmed that Dabney valued his family's reputation more than the lives of innocent women at risk from a serial killer. "I'll never look at Dabney the same way again," she said. She had lost all respect for her fellow Virginian.

The whole afternoon after we met Dabney, we went over our options. We were stuck regarding how to spread the truth about

Uriah Jenkins, his crimes, and his vigilante execution by Colonel Horton.

Nobody would publicize the tale without checking with the Horton family, and Dabney owned or had connections with every media outlet in the state. We knew Dabney meant what he said, about taking every step possible to hinder our purpose. He had doubtless already begun moving Uriah Jenkins' skeleton, and the bones of the hanged slave killer would be thrown into some new anonymous location that would be another Horton family secret.

Throughout the day, Amanda and I talked and talked. I didn't share all of Amanda's pessimism, however. She was crushed by Dabney's non-cooperation. She felt that the whole murder investigation was now at a standstill, that all our work and all the amazing things we'd seen, had come to nothing because of Dabney's obstinacy.

I looked at the situation more pragmatically. For me, I was glad to take a fresh look at our search for the murderer. I wanted to get my feet back on the ground and away from the spirit world, and go back to a focus on modern reality. My thought was to begin re-working the investigation in traditional gumshoe fashion.

Amanda's head, however, was in the world beyond. She was listening for spirits, still eager to communicate with life beyond the grave.

After dinner, we were carrying on our conversations at Amanda's place. It finally got late, and Amanda invited me to sleep on her sofa again. It was just fine for me to spend the night at Amanda's, even if I wasn't sharing her bed.

I went to sleep in Amanda's living room while once again gazing upon the bust of the raven over Amanda's door. I thought about the murdered young women, about the ghost of Uriah, and the big shoot-out where all those people died. *Jesus*, I said to myself, *what a pile of stuff to see and live through!*

I'm usually not very literary, but as I dropped off to sleep I thought of Amanda's ancestor Edgar Allan Poe. I composed in my mind a sort of 'investigative poem' to the meter of Edgar Allan Poe's famous *The Raven*:

Once upon a midnight dreary
While I pondered, weak and weary,
On three young women raped and stabbed
For reasons we know not wherefor;
When suddenly there came while napping
Someone evil who *was* attacking
Attacking my soul's inner core
Quoth this ghost, "Your death's in store!"

    Satisfied with my amateur creative burst, I fell asleep, my mind filled with images of people who were no longer living.

    I was not too long asleep before Amanda woke me. She was sitting on the edge of the sofa where I lay, her delicate hands upon my shoulders, her dark eyes sparkling with starlight. She was smiling, and looked very kissable. But I held myself back, and just gazed affectionately upon her.

    "Get dressed," she said. "We have a very special trip to make."

    I didn't inquire as to the purpose of our expedition, feeling once again in the tow of Amanda's mysterious influence and that I would find things out in due time. I got ready, and then we drove away in Amanda's car. We drove only about a mile, and we parked just off Main Street in the deserted lot next to the Edgar Allan Poe Museum. It was nearly 2 a.m.

"What are we doing here?" I asked.

"I've got a key!" said Amanda.

We opened the door and went inside one of the oldest houses standing in Richmond. Although Edgar Allan Poe did not live in this old stone structure, as far as anyone knows, the house is now a museum in his honor.

The floors creaked loudly in the old house as we walked past the Poe Museum exhibits. Amanda did not turn on any lights; the security lamps slightly above the floor were sufficient to illuminate our way. It was dark and moody and delightful. How wonderful and appropriate, I thought, that Amanda would have snagged her private key to this remarkable place.

My favorite part of the museum – also favorite, it turned out, for Amanda – is the classic walled courtyard that takes up more than half the grounds, a garden courtyard filled with stone benches, ornate pots and other items that give it a truly antique feeling. Whenever I visit the Poe Museum courtyard, I always feel as if I am glimpsing a happy life in a much earlier era.

We proceeded through the courtyard door into the walled garden. It was a lovely warm Virginia night, and so it was comfortable and indeed heavenly to spend some time under the stars in this ancient hideaway on Main Street. Amanda and I got comfortable on a bench, and she encouraged me to put my head in her lap. She caressed my hair and my face with her hand. I didn't know what I had done to earn this special treatment, but I loved every minute of it.

As I looked up at the stars I grew drowsy. Amanda said, "Here's a story from one of my grandfathers," and then began a tale that I do not remember hearing. I saw it, I lived it, or I dreamed it. It went like this.

* * *

It is downtown Richmond, the late 1840s. A large and varied crowd fills the street and a large city square. The throng includes gentlemen and gentlewomen, laborers and merchants, slaves and free blacks. The ages vary from elderly to extremely young.

Looking into the square, one can see the object of the crowd's interest. A public hanging is taking place. The legs of the suspended murderer are just exhibiting the last twitches of life. The silence that greeted the condemned man's initial moments of suffering, has now given way to talk and observation and even laughter. In a few moments the man will be dead.

In the crowd there is a familiar face, a young man with dark hair and a mustache, dressed in the finest styles of the day. He is Uriah Jenkins, a young man who has not yet become a murderer, a young man who still lives at home with his rich Virginia family.

As the body of the hanged man dangles limply in the city breezes, the crowd begins to disperse now that the action in the government-supplied spectacle has ended. Uriah Jenkins himself does not tarry too long after the man's corpse stops swaying. He begins a leisurely stroll through the streets of this fine Southern city.

Not too far from Gallows Square, Uriah sees a man who catches his eye. This other man is dressed shabbily, in dark clothes. He is sitting on the front steps of a house with darkened windows, a house that is not his own. The man has a dark, brooding expression, and he is staring emptily at the pavement.

Despite the man's shabby dress and emotionally troubled countenance, there is something remarkable about him. There is an air of intelligence and dignity, the aura of something remarkable. Uriah speaks to him.

"Good day, sir."

"Good day, sir, to you," says the brooding man on the steps.

"Would you care for a drink at the nearby tavern?" says Uriah. "I'm inclined to share the satisfying of my thirst."

"I would share a table with the Devil himself if he offered me a drink," says the man in the shabby coat.

"We'll invite the Devil, too," says Uriah, delighted with the idea.

The men walk together to the tavern and introduce themselves. The man in the shabby coat is Edgar Allan Poe.

* * *

In the candlelight of the tavern, it is clear that the emaciated Edgar Poe is not only malnourished, but downright sickly. He is grateful for the liquor and food that is provided, but his gratitude does not prevent him from viewing his table companion with an accurate and penetrating gaze.

"I've often wondered what it's like to be hanged," says Uriah Jenkins. "To die slowly at the end of a rope, your fellow citizens watching your final agonies. I wonder if one can think clearly at all in those minutes before death overwhelms the mind."

Edgar Poe is not unduly disturbed by this topic. "I believe," he says, "That it is one of the fascinations of the criminal spirit, to look forward to experiencing the consequences of his crime.

"I think some men kill in part so they can look forward to the sensations of being hanged, an experience that they could boast of as rare and singular, if boast they could from the grave. It may well be that for some criminals, the fascination with execution is the beginning of life outside the law."

Uriah's eyes grow wide and then he smiles. He is enjoying this conversation immensely. "What say you of crime, Mr. Poe? Is it not human nature to delight in crime, to revel in it? Was there a man in the crowd who did not secretly wish some share in the sensations of that murderer in the moment of his misdeed?"

Edgar drinks and stays silent a moment before answering, and he then replies in a personal manner. "I think of crime every day," he says. "My whole life has been tinged with crimes of a petty and minor nature," Edgar confesses. "Evasion of debt, wagering, drunkenness, misconduct and revenge, all these offenses and more have been mine in ample quantity.

"I have seen the inside of a jail cell, and thus I am company with that low and base brethren who have known the wrath of the law. I know that much crime comes from drink and lack of money, two sisters who have been my companions since youth. I still do not have a firm judgement, however, as to whether the criminal impulse is a part of ourselves, or a force emanating from outside of us."

Uriah asks him, "Any inclination toward a larger sort of crime, Mr. Poe?"

"In cases of personal motive," replies the poet, "Yes, indeed. I have felt jealousy and the lust for revenge strongly enough to consider killing, but it is not in me to truly commit such acts. My grander disturbances remain wrapped within my soul, wounding my spirit many times more severely than I am tempted to wound another."

"We are *not* alike, Mr. Poe," answers Uriah. "Wealth has given me immunity from the smaller temptations. I too have been tempted to violence in personal matters, but the temptation there is quick and passing.

261

"What does compel my imagination," Uriah continues, "Are the planning of crimes that are totally, purely *devilish*. Crimes against victims of complete innocence. Crime for its own sake, the very *essence* of crime, that is what I find tempting, tempting beyond all reason!"

The servant brings another ale. Edgar Poe knows he has just heard a confession, and that he is face to face with someone of quite inhuman nature. "Mr. Jenkins, you are a singular man," he says. "I have no doubt you are capable of extraordinary actions."

"I see we understand one another, Mr. Poe," says Uriah, still taking pleasure in the encounter. "The ultimate crime, wouldn't you agree, Mr. Poe, is crime against young womanhood. Would not the greatest intensity of feeling be in inverting those timid affections that habitually go on between male and female? Would not the ultimate pleasure be in rendering young womanhood into a pure object of a man's will?" Uriah's face shows the perverse pleasure he takes in these thoughts.

"Would it not," Uriah continues, "Would it not be the *ultimate* satisfaction to have an unrestrained freedom in working one's whims on a young female, whether that freedom be in physical satiation, or the indulgence of violence, or the imposition of death itself? Is not this the final *delight* which life can offer a few chosen souls?"

Edgar Poe's expression draws dark and even more troubled than usual. He exhales emotionally into his mug of ale. His left hand reaches into his pocket to handle a knife he usually carries with him.

Edgar thinks about how it would be right and good to kill Uriah Jenkins. But despite his clear judgement that Uriah is a monster who will some day perform acts of immense evil, Edgar feels inert and restrained. He sees it is not his role in the world to bring an early end to Uriah Jenkins' life, despite the despicable nature of his being and the horrors he will commit in future years.

For a long time there is silence at this tavern table shared by Edgar Allan Poe and Uriah Jenkins. Uriah smiles perversely and Edgar broods gloomily. Finally, Edgar breaks the silence by talking about love.

"I love womanhood, I worship it," says Edgar. "I have not been a good husband or an equal lover, but my devotion to the feminine is the salvation of my soul. The desires of which *you* speak, Mr. Jenkins, are the desires of demons from hell and not of men." Edgar's strong language surprises even himself. He expects Jenkins to make a move to strike him.

"Why not, Mr. Poe, seek to know personally what Lucifer himself knows?" responds Uriah, surprising Edgar with his calm. Uriah continues, his eyes roving around the room at the serving women and the proprietor's daughter. "Perhaps even some women here could know my iron hand someday. I might be a *god* to them, a god of power and pleasure, a god of pain and death!"

Edgar Poe drinks deeply, and glares at Uriah Jenkins. Edgar wonders why it is the constant curse of his sensitive life, to always be confronted with the worst horrors and darknesses of living.

"What say you of black servitude, Mr. Poe?" asks Uriah. "Is it a way of life that will always be with us?"

Edgar Poe looks around the tavern. "Many of us are slaves, and there are many types of slavery," he replies. "I have been a slave in my own life, at many times and in many ways. I say it is a hopeless dream to think that society will be corrected and made wholesome by eliminating one nefarious institution.

"But," Edgar continues, "I do not think that black servitude will survive many generations. Other forms of servitude will replace it, most likely the crass servitude of money and of overweening government. It is the natural course of things to change, for one form of human domination to come in place of another."

"I know you, Mr. Poe," says Uriah. "You're a scribbler, a literary man. You walk these streets in poverty, and yet you're known across the states of this nation. You write of the dark side of human life, of horrors and nightmares and impulses to madness. I've read some of your tales, and I know you as a great *thinker*. I, however, Mr. Poe, shall one day be a man of *action*, a kind of man about whom you could write.

265

"Let me suggest an idea to you, Mr. Poe," says Uriah, continuing his train of thought. "Why not imagine what slave ownership could become in the hands of a truly bold master? Why not imagine a large house where slaves, and particularly Negro women in youth, are put through the most unspeakable humiliation and torture before expiring at the master's hands? Why not imagine a white woman suffering as a slave, too? Would this not make a truly compelling tale for your pen?"

"Habitually," replies Edgar, "I write of the fantastic, the amazing, the phantasmagorical. The kind of tale of which you speak, while quite a moving and affecting discourse, is too much an accurate tale of Southern living to be subject to my more other-worldly pen." Edgar stares at Jenkins firmly, facing down the rich pervert despite his own ill-health and near-drunken condition.

"Mr. Poe," says Uriah, "You are not going to live many years beyond this one. And while your bones are rotting, I will *satisfy* myself with pleasures so horrific that even *you* would shrink from writing about them. I will make myself into such a demon that these horrors will continue even after I am dead, and women will know *agony* in the service of my ghost! What say you to that, Mr. Poe!"

"I have no doubt you are correct," answers Edgar. "Your ghost will indeed be the taskmaster of torment and fear. But one day your victims will have their final word. They will escort your ghostly carriage to the door of hell, and you will never be heard from again as you strangle forever on the gallows of eternity!"

Uriah stands and places a gold coin on the table. "Drink yourself to death, sir," he says, and he turns to depart.

"I am indebted for the ale and dinner, but this is a debt I shall never pay," says Edgar, as Uriah Jenkins goes on his way. Edgar remains and drinks until he collapses at the table. He awakes before sunrise, and finds himself lying in the street, the stench of Uriah Jenkins' criminal essence still in his nostrils.

* * *

There is one last meeting between Edgar Poe and Uriah Jenkins, some weeks later in the early afternoon. It is near the Slave Quarters building, when Jenkins is loading some newly purchased slaves into a cart for transport back to Louisa county.

A young black mother sits chained in the cart and tries to comfort her small child, and Uriah Jenkins boxes her on the ears just as Edgar Allan Poe is walking up the street.

This sort of public abuse of a slave is not proper in old Virginia society, but it is also considered improper for any other gentleman to intervene. Nonetheless, the frail Edgar runs to lay himself upon Uriah, his fists flailing in helpless fury. A few quick blows from Uriah, and the illustrious poet and author Edgar Allan Poe lies in the gutter, his clothes soiled with dirt and horse manure.

"I'll have my way with women, Mr. Poe!" says Uriah, laughing as he prepares to ride away.

"One day you'll be in hell, Mr. Jenkins!" answers Edgar, getting himself up out of the muck. As the carriage rides forth, the young slave mother in chains looks at Edgar Allan Poe with a warm and tender expression, a look he remembers till the last day of his life.

* * *

These stories of the meetings between Edgar Allan Poe and Uriah Jenkins, are as clearly in my mind as if I had seen them happen. When I awoke with their memory, sunshine was pouring into the courtyard at the Edgar Allan Poe Museum. I was seated on the large bench, and Amanda Poe was cradled in my arms, her features delicate and childlike in her early morning repose.

I gently woke her, and we went back to Amanda's place for coffee and breakfast. Both of us were eager to get back to the work of finding the serial killer, a killer perhaps already scouting the streets for his next tragic victim.

Pain and Death

Sometimes, detective work is a matter of following up on a random series of leads or hunches. Most of the trails go nowhere, but it might only take one lucky lead to crack an entire case.

Amanda was completely depressed about Dabney Horton's enforcement of silence regarding the secrets of the Old Mansion. The way she saw it, we were close to catching a serial murderer. We had discovered the killer's inspiration, his source of perverted nourishment, in the ghostly doings of Uriah Jenkins.

Amanda thought that as soon as we publicized the Jenkins story, she could put her ear to the spiritual winds and we would quickly find the killer. Amanda was sure that as long as Dabney was preventing the truth about Uriah Jenkins from being known to the living, Uriah's *ghost* could prevent the souls of the dead from helping us. In Amanda's view, we were completely stuck.

I'm never a guy to give up. After long discussion, Amanda finally agreed to resume the murder investigation on a more earthly, ordinary level. I would take the lead, and we would follow up on any clue or pathway that seemed remotely helpful.

We considered going over the ground already covered by the regular police investigators. We thought we might catch something the cops had missed. The process of duplicating the steps of dozens of police officers, however, would be a long and slow one, and we feared the killer might have time to murder more victims before we were finished.

Our best hope of getting to the murderer before he killed anyone else, was in thinking of some fresh avenues to pursue.

We were in Amanda's kitchen talking things over. Amanda started talking about her depression over Dabney again. "I hate having my hands tied like this," said Amanda. "Damn that Dabney Horton and all his money and power, damn him."

"Hands tied," I repeated. "Amanda, you've given me an idea," I said.

She looked puzzled for a second, and then she picked up my thought. "That sado-masochism club that we learned about at that kinky store at Slave Quarters, that sold the whips and paddles and shackles! If the killer likes to bind up and torment people, he might be a club member or at least a visitor!"

"Exactly," I said. "I remember the brochure, it was called the 'Different Strokes Club'. Do you have a copy of *Style* magazine? There's probably a listing and number in there."

Style is a free Richmond weekly that has a lot of advertisements for entertainment, and listings for personal ads and sexual connections. Sure enough, near the personal ads was a small blurb for the 'Different Strokes Club', which described its members' interests as including "bondage, whipping, spanking, piercing, branding, pain and punishment, light to medium strength, in a lingerie and high heels, leather and lace atmosphere". The ad repeated the slogan we remembered from the brochure about "Safe and Wild Sex for the Nineties".

We called the number in the ad and there was a long recording which began by saying, "You are so *bad* to be calling us . . ." The recording went on to describe the Different Strokes Club and invite anyone who wanted to learn more, or attend an event, to leave a voice-mail message. Amanda left a reply requesting a call back:

"Hi, my name is Amanda, and my boyfriend has been saying he'd like to whip me. I'm starting to fantasize about being tied up and punished, so I'd like to find out more about the Club and maybe my boyfriend and I can attend an event and maybe I can overcome some of my inhibitions." She then left her phone number on the tape.

I was trying to control my giggles while Amanda was on the phone. "You do want to whip me, don't you?" she teased me. "We'll have to make this at least a little *real* if we go to a Club party." I laughed and didn't say anything.

Within an hour we got a call from a charming man with a British accent. He talked to us a little about the Club, about our own level of interest, and what we might expect at a Club event. There was a Club gathering the very next evening, and when we expressed a strong interest in attending he gave us a full interview regarding ourselves, took our names and addresses, and went over the rules that governed conduct at this sex-and-punishment party.

He gave us numerous cautions regarding safe sex and respect for others, and clearly warned against any real violence that does 'permanent harm'.

We were surprised when our caller gave us an address in Richmond's wealthy Windsor Farms neighborhood as the site of the Different Strokes Club party, which would begin after sunset.

It seemed possible that we might meet our killer through this sado-masochistic sex club. A psychopath whose greatest pleasure was in killing and tormenting helpless women, *might* associate himself with a club devoted to people who like to play domination games.

275

Amanda and I knew, of course, that most people engaged in the sexual domination hobby are harmless good citizens. But it seemed logical we could pick up a lead by mixing with people who enjoy using slave-shackles for intimate entertainment.

* * *

On our way to the Different Strokes Club social event, Amanda and I had one of those strange conversations about sex that sometimes take place between people who aren't yet lovers, but who someday might be in bed together.

"What do you think of S&M?" said Amanda, who was sitting next to me in my car and wearing a spicy black outfit: Black bra underneath a short unbuttoned jacket, leather miniskirt and wicked spike heels. Around her neck was a jeweled choker, and she wore marvelous glittery earrings.

For my part, I had on a black short-sleeve cotton shirt and gray jeans, which was exactly as wild as *I* cared to appear. I didn't want to be mistaken for someone overeager for S&M foreplay.

"S&M?" I said. "I definitely would not be a serious S&M person. I think you look good in black, though, *especially* the black underwear. How about you?" I asked. "Any desires for dominance?"

"I'm not really the S&M club type, either. Though sometimes I like the idea of being strong and in control, and sometimes I like the idea of being under someone else's complete control, too. You know what I mean?"

I nodded as if I did follow her completely, which I didn't.

Amanda continued: "I think sex can be partly about power," she said. "And I think it can be fun to play with that idea. Not to the point of the S&M groupies, but just to where you can feel the flow and interchange of strength and submission. You understand that, don't you?"

I just grinned like a dummy. "I like you Amanda, I really do," I said.

* * *

At the door of the spacious colonial house in Richmond's exclusive Windsor Farms neighborhood, we were met by our hostess, Felicity Monroe, an attractive woman of about 50 with short dark hair. She was dressed in a leather bra and panties, garter belt and heels. She looked silly, her outfit a little unsuited to her age and station in life. But her costuming herself in this way made her seem appealingly vulnerable as well.

Felicity had a clipboard in her hand. "Amanda, I don't know if you remember meeting me."

"Of course, Felicity," said Amanda. "It was about five years ago, a fundraising party at the Valentine Museum."

"How sweet that you remember," said Felicity, the well-mannered Virginia lady in leather panties.

It was about 9:30pm and the party was in full gear in Felicity's expansive home. The large living room had been turned into a dance floor, and the crowd was in a good mood. About half the folks were dressed normally, about half in some form of S&M costume. Couples of all ages danced together, some of them couples of the same sex. A few danced with small whips, and gently lashed their partners as they danced. Two dancers held on to chains fastened to their partners' clothing.

As newcomers, we were assigned a guide to the proceedings. Our guide turned out to be Gillian Trumbull, a mathematics professor at one of the colleges in town. Gillian went over the ground rules of the party, talking about safe sex and respect for others. He invited us to masturbate or have intercourse in any of the smaller rooms of the house.

As we walked through the house, we saw a number of dominance scenes being enacted. A woman was tied to a four-poster bed. People were being whipped, caned, and paddled. Some were having sex in rooms with open doors, seemingly inviting others to watch and review.

I didn't understand the idea of having sex before a large group of gawking strangers. But it was, after all, the 'Different Strokes Club'.

Then, in one room, I saw something that genuinely disturbed me. A small young woman who seemed to be a teenage girl, was chained to the frame of a brass bed, lying across it on her stomach. Her blouse was ripped, her bra was up around her shoulders, her blue jeans and panties were down around her ankles.

Standing behind her was a somewhat ugly man wearing silver studs on his belt. Just as Amanda and I reached the doorway to see in, the man lashed her bottom with a cat-o'-nine-tails. The young girl yelped; there were tears in her eyes. Amanda and I rushed in. I knelt down to talk to the girl. Amanda stood behind, seeing what damage was done to her backside and gazing upon the man that had whipped her.

I looked into the eyes of the crying and helpless girl. She seemed about fifteen. "How old are you?" I asked, speaking as tenderly as I could.

"Oh, I'm twenty-six," she said. "I know, I look about twelve," she continued, her tears subsiding. "Believe it or not, I'm a lawyer," she continued, smiling through her tears. "I need to get my bottom whipped sometimes, I'm such a bad girl."

Our tour guide Gillian whispered something to the man with the cat-o'-nine-tails. "Judy," he then said to the chained girl, "I know you need your ass whipped, but that cat-o'-nine-tails is rough. Should we get something milder?"

"No," said Judy. "You can whip me once or twice more," she said, sniffling.

"Can I masturbate on you?" said the man.

"Just leave me chained up while you do it," said Judy.

Amanda and I left the room. This was pretty *raw* stuff I was seeing. I didn't know what to think.

"I'm not denying that things get out of hand here sometimes," said Gillian. "But really it's all in good fun. That's Roy who was doing the beating there. He's really a sweet guy."

"Do you ever worry," asked Amanda, "Whether some of the things you do here contribute to real violence? Could some criminal get encouraged or inspired by seeing this kind of domination of women, for example?"

"No, I don't think so," answered Gillian. "I don't think that people who fully accept their

S&M sexuality are even *capable* of being criminals. Everybody here sees S&M as foreplay, as sex, as fun and games. When you make S&M your hobby, that means you know it's not real and it shouldn't be real.

"It's not our Club members who beat their kids and attack people on the street. It's the people who are repressed, who *haven't* explored their sexual fantasies of dominance and submission, it's *those* people who become criminals, abusers, rapists and murderers. I think when you admit your own S&M sexuality – and there's a little S&M in *all* of us – I think you're on your way to being a free, liberated and good person."

* * *

We spent another forty-five minutes at the Different Strokes Club party, making the rounds and observing the goings-on, but both Amanda and I came to the feeling that there was no trace of our killer in the Club. Despite the S&M atmosphere, the make-believe violence, and the preoccupation with pain and dominance, the whole party was so socially upscale and cheery that it seemed quite unconnected to the real violence of a serial killer.

Amanda could feel no trace of anything genuinely criminal or evil among the group, and she was sure she could have felt if anyone there had even known the killer.

So, our curiosity satisfied, we excused ourselves from the party and got ready to depart. On our way out, we saw Judy, the teen-age-looking lawyer who had been crying earlier while being whipped. She was wearing just her bra and blue jeans and dancing happily in the living room. She smiled and waved at us as we left.

On the way home I asked Amanda if she thought that Gillian might be right, that the S&M sexual outlet channeled the impulses of people in a safe way and actually *prevented* people from being more vicious in the world. "For some people, yes. For others, I wouldn't be sure of that," she replied. "But I did feel sure that there were no killers involved with the Different Strokes Club. There were no psychic footprints of any murderers, not even a whiff of Uriah Jenkins."

I nodded. It had been a good idea to explore the town's kinky sex club, but it wasn't the road we needed to take.

* * *

Central Virginia is filled with Civil War battlefields. Perhaps the most moving of these sites is the remaining trenches of Cold Harbor, where General Grant's misjudgement resulted in the swiftest military massacre ever seen up to that point in human history.

Early one June morning in 1864, the Union troops made a final assault on the Confederate position at Cold Harbor, just a few miles northeast of downtown Richmond. The Confederates were much better prepared than the Union commanders had realized. From their secure positions in the trenches, the Southerners mowed down row after row of blue-uniformed Union troops.

In a matter of a few minutes, several thousand Union soldiers were shot down. The air of the dawn was filled with the roar of gunfire and the screams of thousands of maimed and dying men. It was the world's first experience of how trench warfare could yield quick and colossal carnage. It was a prelude to the millions of lives lost in the trenches of World War I.

The death of thousands of men within a matter of minutes at Cold Harbor, was the result of what General Grant considered his greatest mistake and failure of the Civil War. It was also the last great Southern victory of that War, and is still celebrated as such to this day by citizens of the former Confederacy.

The trenches at Cold Harbor extended over several miles in 1864, but only a few hundred feet of those trenches remain intact today, preserved in a national historical park. Those short stretches of battleground, however, still evoke a vivid impression of the masses of men fighting and dying on that fateful June morning in 1864.

You stand at the Confederate position, and see the Union earthworks a few hundred feet across a field. Instantly, you can feel the presence of the men who fought and expired there. You almost can hear the gunfire and the screams. You know that the short distance between the combatants, short enough to traverse in a few seconds of running, was the route to eternity for thousands of dying soldiers who gave their lives trying to run against a rainstorm of fat lead bullets.

Everyone who sees Cold Harbor Battlefield today comes away touched by the souls of the men who killed and died on that ground. It is one of the few places where, even before I met Amanda Poe, I can remember feeling in contact with the spirits of the dead.

As Amanda and I continued our search for the serial killer inspired by Uriah Jenkins, she and I went back to Cold Harbor together, hoping there might be a connection between the violent deaths of the past and the blood spilled in the present.

* * *

Amanda and I wondered whether the serial killer at large in Virginia might be someone who was obsessed with the Southern past. Given that this killer was in contact with the ghost of a 19th century slave-murderer, we thought we might turn up a clue by looking among those who made a hobby out of re-enacting aspects of Confederate life.

The past of Virginia, like the past of any Southern state, is in part a history of violence: Slavery and its tortures, racism and its indignities, the Ku Klux Klan and its lynchings. The rebellion against the North killed hundreds of thousands of people, with as much blood spilled in Virginia as anywhere. Amanda and I thought that a killer attracted to themes of blood and violence, might well have a more than casual interest in Virginia history.

There was a special event taking place at Cold Harbor battlefield that Amanda and I hoped would be a chance to pick up a lead for our investigation. Civil War re-enactors in full period uniforms were re-staging the bloody Battle of Cold Harbor for film cameras sponsored by public television.

The Virginia societies of Civil War re-enactors were dedicated and even fanatical in their devotion to realism. They used perfectly authentic uniforms and weapons, blood-curdling battle yells, aggressive field tactics, and were more than willing to scream and fake death as part of their commitment to stage a battle as realistically as possible.

Due to the filming of the scene, the re-enactment was closed to the general public, but there were many historical society observers present, and Amanda and I gained admission with our state police credentials.

Although the real Battle of Cold Harbor took place in the early morning, the filming and re-enactment was done in mid-afternoon. As the hundreds of authentically-dressed volunteers prepared for the mock battle, Amanda and I walked among them, looking for someone who might give us a clue or perhaps even be the killer himself.

It was quite an impressive group. Those dressed as Confederate soldiers took their Civil War imagery seriously. Even the smallest details, including their hairstyles and mustaches, aped the look of men documented by old photographs.

A couple of the men had faces vaguely reminiscent of Uriah Jenkins, and brought to my mind the ghostly image that had appeared to me in the window of the haunted Old Mansion.

Amanda and I moved among the group in silence, watching and observing. There was a feel of profundity in the air, almost as if the upcoming battle would be a real one, though we could see or sense nothing that seemed helpful to our search for the murderer.

The battle area was cleared of onlookers, the cameras began rolling, and the well-planned battle re-creation began. The Union soldiers shouted and charged, the blackpowder rifles began to roar, and soon the air was dense with white smoke. Within seconds, the Union front line lay scattered across the field, some of the men writhing and screaming. It was effectively and somewhat horribly realistic.

The Union soldiers charged again, and more bodies joined those already on the ground. New screams filled the air as others were reduced to silence or low moaning. The Confederates reloaded, more bluecoats charged, and once again great numbers of the living were reduced to heaps of bodies of the seemingly dead.

The white smoke of blank-shooting weapons soon filled the air to the point that little could be seen, though the gunfire and screams could still be heard. Finally, the shooting mostly stopped, and the smoke cleared a little. It was even more awful now that the screams of the wounded echoed by themselves. Bodies were piled sometimes three or four deep, the wounded sometimes lying in vocal agony with the silent dead crushing them from above.

It was a triumphant display of re-enactment realism. Those of us observing were in awe; we felt almost as if we had witnessed a real battle.

The filming over, the 'dead and wounded' arose and the bluecoats and gray uniforms shook hands and headed for the picnic tables. The atmosphere was cordial, with mutual respect for all those who had fought and died in the War Between the States.

Amanda and I circulated among the throng at the picnic, chatting and talking with many. We found a great many interesting and appealing individuals. No one seemed attracted to violence for its own sake; just about all were pervaded with respect for the courage and commitment of our ancestors, and compassion for those who suffered and perished.

"How do you think those Confederate soldiers felt, shooting and mowing down all those Union soldiers like so many turkeys?" asked Amanda, speaking to a young man in wire-rimmed glasses, holding a drink in one hand, and his big-bore antique rifle in the other.

"It was a terrible loss for the North, and the Confederacy did not suffer many losses in the battle, that's true," said the young man. "But those men in the Southern trenches were still heroes, despite the advantages they had in this encounter.

"They were ready to die where they stood," the young man continued. "They were the same men who risked everything at Spotsylvania, at Petersburg, at Appomattox. It was carnage, but it was not bloodlust. It was men defending their homes and what they saw as a true American Constitution. I was proud today to be able just to stand where they stood."

Amanda and I nodded. I complimented the young man's dress and bearing and the day's collective work, and we moved on. Both Amanda and I understood that the murderer would not be anywhere near here. There was too much respect, too much reverence, for a cold sadistic killer to be a part of this group.

We had to think again about where to look for a murderer.

Flight of the Raven

After a few more days of following up on ideas and hunches that proved fruitless, Amanda and I went to dinner one night at the Church Hill Café near where we lived. Our meal was made somber by our mutual sense of foreboding.

It had been several weeks since the murderer had claimed his last victim and dumped her body by a country road near the Old Mansion. Both Amanda and I felt that the time was drawing nigh when this killer would select another victim from the young women of Richmond. The clock was ticking, and if we did not find the killer soon, another young woman would almost certainly be dead.

I myself was coming to think that Amanda's mystical connections to the spirit world really had been our best route to catching the murderer. In our visions at the Old Mansion, we had seen the same ghost, the ghost of Uriah Jenkins, that this unknown killer was seeing in *his* perverted dreams.

I thought Amanda was probably right. If the millionaire Dabney Horton had let Amanda follow through on the plan to publicize the Uriah Jenkins story, and thus evaporate the power held by Uriah's ghost, we would probably already have the killer in custody.

As we had coffee and dessert, Amanda seemed to develop some new inspiration. "You know, David, I think it's wonderful how you've wanted to keep on going in this case, even though we haven't had a concrete direction to take. To hell with Dabney Horton! I think I shouldn't have given up so quickly on finding a spiritual pathway to solving these murders.

"I think," she said, continuing, "That we should go back to Hollywood Cemetery tonight, and spend some time by the grave of Cassandra Williams. Even if Uriah's ghost won't let her speak freely, we have done enough work finding the truth about Uriah Jenkins that he might not be able to silence the spirits of the victims entirely. If we're patient, the innocent dead might be able to help us, even if we can't get the whole story.

"We might be able to pick up *something*, some hint, some image, that'll help us locate the killer. The killer is in Richmond somewhere, and even a partial clue might help us nab him.

I nodded. "I bet he lives in one of the older neighborhoods, too," I said, "The Fan or Church Hill or Northside or Shockoe Bottom. I don't think he's in suburbia. He probably lives in a house that goes back to the last century."

"I think you're right," she agreed. I did not have Amanda's mystical powers, but I could feel that our instincts were falling more into unison as our time together continued.

* * *

Dusk was falling as we entered the gate to Richmond's ancient cemetery, in the heart of the old city. The iron latch clanged shut behind us as we prepared for another evening amid graves and ghosts. It was very warm for this late in the day, as is typical in Virginia as spring fades into summer. The air in the cemetery was sweet and pleasant with the scent of flowers newly in bloom.

With flashlights in hand, and sleeping bags and knapsacks on our backs, we made our way to the grave of Cassandra Williams, who had been the first young woman known to die at the hands of the killer some three months ago. We stood for a moment in silence by the obviously fresh grave, its headstone gleaming with the sheen of freshly polished marble.

Amanda and I sat down by the graveside and got comfortable. We were mostly quiet. Amanda affirmed that her ability to communicate with the dead victim seemed just as stifled as before. She felt that the victim wanted to tell her something, but that the voice could not be heard in her mind. Amanda thought, however, that if we were willing to spend the entire night by the grave, we might come to the morning with some image or information we could use.

As I looked around at the endless and uneven rows of gravestones, I thought about how my impression of a cemetery was so different now that I knew Amanda Poe. A cemetery now seemed much more interesting. I had a variety of sensations, partly comforting and partly fearful, feelings as diverse as the kinds of people who were buried there in the ground beneath us. I felt myself amid a legion of personalities. Sleeping, dormant, *dead* personalities, to be sure; but personalities nonetheless!

Night came to the cemetery. The historic Hollywood cemetery was closed to the public after dark, and so we were alone. Traffic could be heard on the streets surrounding, but we were at least a quarter mile away from the nearest perimeter. We were, indeed, alone with the dead.

Soon we began to get drowsy, with that drowsiness I now recognized as being not from tiredness or sleepiness, but a drowsiness that is a gateway to contact with the spirits of the departed.

Amanda and I had the same dreams: There were dreams of riding in a car, a car being driven endless miles through the streets of Richmond. The dream view was from the back seat, a large and spacious back seat, like in a full-sized car, with dark cloth upholstery.

In these dreams, I was looking out the car window dazedly at the passing houses and streetlamps of nighttime Richmond. Whenever I woke from these dreams, I closed my eyes so that I could quickly fall back into the dream and learn more.

I wanted especially to look into the front seat of the car and see who was driving. But every time the dream returned, I could only see the back seat of the car and the passing view outside the window. Amanda had the same experience.

At one point in the night, Amanda and I awoke at the same time, and we held each other close, cheek to cheek, both of us swept with a feeling of dread. In our dreams, we had seen a tragic house from the inside: Peeling plaster, narrow rooms, and small and crookedly constructed doorways, marking a modest 19th century-style Richmond townhouse after decades of neglect.

In our dreams of this house we saw no people, but we felt ourselves moving through the house and down its stairways. In the basement was a musty room and a set of shackles attached to an old brick wall, a wall stained with dried blood.

This was the murderer's torture chamber where three women had recently died! We had now seen the interior of the house of the murderer. If only we could get a clue to the outside!

After comforting one another, Amanda and I almost forced ourselves back to sleep, to see if we could pick up a clue, any clue, that would help pin down the location of the killer. We barely had our eyes closed, when they seemed to open again, and we both appeared to be wide awake. We were looking away from Cassandra's grave across the starlit cemetery, and we suddenly felt a powerful force of warmth and love behind us. We turned around in our sleeping bags to see a beautiful young woman standing barefoot on the grave. Her clothing was a torn and crude garment, but her body and face glowed with a beauty that suggested perfection. We both recognized her as Cassandra, the murder victim who was buried beneath the freshly laid dirt.

"Thank you," said Cassandra, in a voice that was sincere and sweet. "I wish I could help you more," she added, and then she lay down on top of her own grave and seemed to go to sleep. My own eyes fell shut, too.

When I woke next I found myself standing up, and I was pointing my loaded pistol at a man in front of me. Amanda was standing up, too, right behind me.

The man in front of me wore an open-necked shirt, and on his neck were a circle of ugly red marks. His eyes bulged, and his swollen tongue protruded from under his mustache as he spoke. "I'm going to kill *again*," the man said. "You Virginians hanged me, but I'm still out killing women. I'm going to find a young Negro girl, and I'm going to slash her and rape her and kill her by cutting her to pieces. I'm going to have my pleasure in her blood and her screams.

"And *you*?" he demanded, his evil eyes piercing into mine, "*You* are going to try and stop me. Hah! Shoot, you fucking bastard, shoot!"

I held my gun firmly and faced down the ghost of Uriah Jenkins, but I did not shoot. "You're right not to shoot," said Amanda, quietly. "A bullet won't work on him now that he's a ghost. But we'll see him quiet, once and for all, and he'll dangle from a tree for eternity."

The ghost of Uriah Jenkins screamed, and then he seemed to both evaporate and charge at us at the same time. A cold, smelly wave of noxious wind blew past me and knocked Amanda right onto the ground. Uriah's departing scream faded into the distance.

Amanda was shaken but all right. We talked about what we had seen and then we tried to go to sleep again, but found that we couldn't. It seemed we had learned all we could at Cassandra's gravesite.

We left the cemetery before dawn with a sense of urgency. The killer, we both felt, was about to kill again. He would be motivated and inspired by the devilish spirit of Uriah Jenkins. The murderer might be only hours away from selecting his next feminine target.

* * *

All through the next day, I had a feeling of anxiety. I was growingly sure that another murder was about to happen. I napped a little at lunchtime, and in my sleep I saw once again the ghost of Uriah Jenkins and the images of murdered women.

Upon awakening, I went over every aspect of the case, trying to formulate a plan or shortcut for finding the murderer. I came up with nothing, except a feeling of dread and imminent disaster.

Just after dark, Amanda and I met at her house, which seemed particularly dark and gloomy tonight. I felt the presence of ghosts in the streets outside, but I was in no fear of the supernatural. I had a nauseous sensation about the fact a killer was on the loose, and that Amanda and I were responsible for finding him before he could kill again.

"What are we going to do?" I asked Amanda.

She got up from her antique love-seat. Her shoulders moved eerily as she rose into the air. "We've got to look, to hunt," she replied. "That's all there is to it. We've got to scour the city, all the old neighborhoods, Church Hill, the Fan, Northside, Blackwell, the Bottom. We've got to find the footsteps of that murderer."

"What are we looking for?" I asked.

"I'm not sure," she answered. "We've gotten a few things from last night by Cassandra's grave. An old house – we know the inside at least. The back seat of a big car driving around the city.

"Anyway, we're not going to find him by sitting in here and thinking about it. We've got to go and look, everywhere possible."

I nodded. "Should we go together?" I asked.

"No. We need to look separately. We'll cover a lot more, and one of us might see something first."

"How'll we stay in touch? You still don't have a car phone. I've got mine reinstalled thanks to Dabney Horton, so do you want to check in with me every two hours or so?"

Amanda smiled. "David, you should *know* by now. When one of us sees something, the other will just *feel* it and head in the right direction." She put her hand on my shoulder and I felt a dark tingle. I touched her hand, and it was cold but deeply affecting; I felt as if I was caressing a wild animal.

I headed out into the night, to drive the streets to look for the killer. Amanda said she would go out not long after I did.

I got in my car and drove a block, and then I decided to circle around through the alley in back of Amanda's townhouse. I moved the car slowly through the old cobblestone by-way. The lights in Amanda's house were out, but the small window to the kitchen was open, its ancient iron grid frame silhouetted in the moonlight.

I felt a cold wind, and all of a sudden a large bird appeared, flying out of Amanda's house. The bird gave a strange cry, and then circled above my car before flying high into the distance above the city. My body felt all a-tingle.

I felt as if something magical had happened, but I was too serious of mind to stay and ponder what I had seen. My task was to find a killer amid this beautiful Southern city, a killer who was still guarded by a ghost from hell.

* * *

Even as the evening started, I knew it would be a long night. I drove around the old streets of Richmond, wearied both by my difficult task and the general evil of humanity. My wits and senses were very sharply attuned, and in surveying Richmond's old neighborhoods, I felt that three centuries had been time for a lot of hate and death to accumulate in its avenues.

I felt myself part of a classic and eternal struggle, the good guys against the bad guys. Thus it always was, and thus it always will be, whether it was riding on a horse with a sword or riding in a car with a gun.

During the course of the evening I felt I drove up and down nearly every old street in the city. My nerves were tense, and at times I could feel my heart pounding. The killer of three young women was somewhere nearby. I prayed for the chance to confront him, to have an opportunity to capture him or shoot him down before he killed again.

At some point, I was probably driving right in front of his house. But where exactly? I only hoped I could find or figure it out soon enough to save the next potential victim.

As I briefly crossed downtown on the overhead highway, I was overtaken with an unusually vivid mental impression of the city. I seemed to see the whole of Richmond from up in the sky, even though I had never taken a helicopter ride or airplane tour over the city.

This image stayed with me as I continued to carefully prowl the streets. My car was moving slowly so as not to miss any potential clue, but I seemed to always know my location from a vantage point up in the sky.

Just before midnight I saw a body laying in the street in the heart of the old Manchester neighborhood, a bustling shopping district forty years ago, but now a storefront ghetto. I got out of my car and approached the corpse-like figure on the ground.

Nearby stood a number of low-life drug-culture types, none of them moving a finger to assist. I snapped off the safety on the fully-loaded pistol beneath my jacket.

The body turned out to be alive, an old man who had collapsed but was still breathing. I went back to my car to call for help, and then went to see what I could do for the old gent. He revived consciousness as I rolled him over.

"Am I dead yet?" he said.

"No, not yet!" I said, laughing a little. "But help is on the way, old fellow."

"Another heart attack, I think," he said. "I thought this was it. I'm ready to go. Thanks, buddy, for stopping – none of these creeps around here gives a shit. I'm 72 years old and I've had it, just had it, seen it all. I think you young folks have a tough world to live in."

"I know what you mean," I said, cradling the old man's shoulders.

"This neighborhood was a great place once. I fell in love here and I was never able to leave, even with all the drugs and the crime. My wife's dead now, but I still remember her, walking along Hull Street with me, holding my hand. I remember it just like it was yesterday.

"I'm gonna die soon, probably right here on the street, just like this, with a bunch of hoodlums looking over my body while I cough up blood and puke."

I didn't say anything, I just held him.

"I'll tell you one thing, though, young man. Love is forever. None of the rest of it matters. Shit. I'm having trouble breathing." He began to pant heavily, and just then the ambulance rolled up with a police unit.

The medics got the man into the stretcher. "Take care, sonny," he said.

"You too," I answered.

I moved on into the night, continuing to search for some sign of a serial killer.

* * *

Towards 2am, while skirting the edges of downtown, I happened upon a robbery. I saw two young suburbanites walking down the street, a couple who had strayed a little too far in search of free parking while engaged in the evening's revels. This young man and woman walked along in obvious ignorance of their environment, easy targets for whatever crooks might be nearby.

And crooks there were. I saw in my rear view mirror that two men emerged from a stairwell and moved toward the couple with obvious criminal intent. The suburbanites, having had a few drinks and oblivious to their surroundings, took no evasive action.

I used my car phone to call the police and moved quickly to circle the block. By the time my call was done and I came around the street again, the suburban couple was being held at knifepoint. I shut off my car's lights and rolled silently toward the scene of the crime. I drew my pistol and emerged from my car.

"I've got a gun, and I'm a private citizen ready to shoot!" I shouted. The two criminals dropped their knives and the woman's purse which they'd already grabbed.

"On your knees, or I'll blow your heads off!" I commanded. I approached them and kicked away the knives on the ground. I continued to aim my pistol at them while we all waited for the police.

The suburban man whom I'd rescued passed gas and wet his pants while he stared at me holding my gun.

"Are you two all right?" I asked the couple.

"No! We've been robbed!" screamed the young woman. Her purse was safely on the ground in front of her, but she was still too stunned to pick it up.

I began to laugh a little. The robbery was upsetting for the suburbanites, but the situation was now comical and minor for an ex-cop like myself.

"How long before the police get here?" said the young man.

"There's the sirens now," I said. "These crooks'll be glad to see that blue light because they know I'm a lot more likely to shoot them than the cops."

"Oh my God," said the young woman.

"Christ, I hope those fuckers get here soon," said one of the crooks.

"Me too," said the other crook.

"Shaddup," I said.

The cops came and collected the human garbage, and after making some statements I was allowed to continue. I remembered what it was like when I had been a policeman, and I saw stuff like this every week. For the citizens who had been robbed or attacked, it was one of the worst experiences of their life.

For the police, however, it was just one more item on the report, one more scummy event in a night's work. Crime is shockingly routine in a world half gone to hell.

* * *

For a while after the robbery I simply continued to drive the dark and empty streets of Richmond, although I don't have a clear recall of much of that time before dawn. I was driving in my car, but my memory is as if I was flying over the city, surveying Richmond from above the rooftops.

My memory comes into focus, however, as I recall being on a deserted street and glancing at my car's clock: It was 3:52am.

I lowered my car's window to let in the fresh air to help keep me awake. A couple of blocks later, I suddenly heard a woman's voice, moaning and begging in the night:

"Don't kill me, don't cut me," said the woman very clearly. A man mumbled something I couldn't make out. I couldn't see the couple yet.

I parked my car, drew my gun and got out. I walked toward the sounds, just around the corner of an abandoned building and beside a set of bushes.

A young man wearing no pants was on top of a mostly naked woman. He held a knife in his hand. The woman's skirt and panties were around her ankles, and her top and bra were about her shoulders. The young man was too involved in his rape to hear me approach.

"No, not this time!" I said, as I placed the cold barrel-bushing of my pistol against the young man's neck. The young man froze. I grabbed the wrist of his hand that held the knife and he dropped it. The man remained on his knees, the woman beneath him.

"Do you know him?" I asked the young woman.

She began to cry with relief. "I know him," she said. "He's evil. Please kill him, can you? Please kill him, I won't tell. He said he was gonna cut my titties off!"

I felt my trigger finger get itchy. I wanted to kill him. I wanted to shoot, to feel the blast and smell the fired gunpowder. I wanted to send the hollowpoint bullet into the rapist's brain and terminate all the evil that was in him. But I also knew what was right.

"I wish I could, but you know I can't," I said to the young woman, apologetically.

"He's gonna get out of jail and come after me," said the young woman, absolutely despondent that the law enforcement system would not protect her.

I spoke to the young rapist. "Let me tell you what I'm gonna do. I'm gonna grab you by the collar and we're gonna walk over to my car. If you twitch, I'm gonna put this 9 millimeter expanding hollowpoint into your brain and you'll be dead. But if I don't kill you now, I'm gonna follow up on you. You know what that means?"

"No, man, no, I don't know," said the rapist with no pants, now a nervous remnant of his former knife-wielding self.

"What that means," I told him, "Is that if you get out of jail and bother this young woman again, I'm not gonna have you arrested. I'm gonna come see you and blow your dick off while you watch. So you're not going to bother this woman again, are you?"

"No, no, man, I ain't never gonna bother her no more," he promised.

"Good," I said, "Now let's see if you can walk over to my car without me having to kill you."

We went over to my car, and for the third time this night I called for help. Although I had caught a rapist with a knife, it was also clear that this was not the serial killer for whom I was searching. The killer I was looking for did his work in an indoor torture chamber, and not in the bushes in the ghetto.

My reporting to the police took up most of the time until dawn, when I headed for

Amanda's. I drove through her alley again and saw a large dark bird perched in her kitchen window, looking in my direction. Was this the same bird that had taken flight from her house last evening?

I drove around to the front and walked up the steps to knock on Amanda's door. After a minute Amanda opened the door in her nightgown, smiling. She kissed me on the cheek, but her lips were ice cold.

When we got inside I looked at the stone bust of the raven above her doorway, and then I walked into the kitchen. The iron-framed window was now closed. I turned around and looked at her.

She smiled knowingly.

"I won't ask," I said.

"Yes, don't ask," she replied, mystically but sweetly.

"We didn't find him," I said, half questioningly.

"Maybe tonight," she said. "Maybe tonight we will."

Woman in Shackles

Amanda and I prepared for a second night of touring the Richmond streets by resting during the daytime. Just before dusk I made my way to Amanda's house so we could coordinate the night's activities. When Amanda greeted me at her door she was wearing a black veil.

"Are you in mourning?" I asked.

"Maybe for us," she replied. I saw she was serious.

"We're going to find him," she asserted, with unearthly confidence. "Maybe tonight, maybe tomorrow. But we will meet him. And one of us might die."

"You don't know?" I queried.

"No. I can feel that we'll find him, but what will happen afterwards is totally unforeseeable."

"Will we be able to stop him from killing any more women?"

"That's something else I don't know. Maybe someone is getting tortured to death right now."

"We better get started," I said.

"Keep your mobile phone on line," she told me. "I got a mini-phone today to carry in my purse, here's the number. We'll need to be in touch in an instant when things happen."

"Right," I replied.

* * *

We once again began separate journeys about the city. Our first hours of touring the streets were uneventful, except for an increasing foreboding of evil that was felt by both of us.

About ten o'clock Amanda and I had a rendezvous for coffee and donuts. I found my appetite was intact despite our mutual sense that we would soon find the serial killer, and perhaps risk our lives in the confrontation.

As we left the donut shop I had an eerie feeling I could not define at first. I realized later that my sense of time had begun to slow down – not quite as slow as in the two gunfights I'd survived, but slow and ponderous nonetheless.

We turned down a dark street where our cars were parked, and we walked along as briskly as we could, our senses sharp and aware. At the cross street in front of us a taxicab crossed through the intersection, and Amanda and I were almost blown over by a strange blast of cold, foul air. It was a blast from hell. Both Amanda and I knew instantly that the killer had just crossed our path.

We ran to the corner as fast as we could, but our motions seemed nightmarishly slow. We got to the corner just in time to see the taillights signal a turn. My own car was just a few yards back. We ran to it and got in.

I turned the key and began to drive. Carefully but hurriedly, I raced around the corner and rode the rear lights of a slow-moving minivan, trying to follow the taxicab ahead up the street, a taxicab which we believed had a murderer inside of it.

Until I had met Amanda Poe and came to know her strange mystical powers, I would never have believed that one could solve a crime or catch a bad guy with any means other than hard, scientific police work, or just plain luck. Now, however, not only did I appreciate her special powers, but I myself was beginning to develop the same kind of intuition. It was intuition that would not stand up in court, but was more than enough to get us going in the right direction.

I thought of Dabney Horton, the stubborn millionaire who had hired us. We might be about to have the killer in our hands. It could soon be time to call him with the news, provided we were alive to tell it.

My car turned the corner that the taxicab had turned, and as soon as I got fully onto the new street I saw the taxi in the distance making another turn. Traffic was thick, but hopefully we would not lose the tail, or tip off the taxi's occupants.

We followed the taxi through two more turns, but always a knot of cars remained between us, blocking closer pursuit along Richmond's narrow streets. Neither Amanda or I knew the terrible truth at that moment, that the taxi ahead of us not only contained the killer, but also his next victim who was being prepared for a torturous death.

The taxi was headed for the highway, where I felt confident I could close in. Just before getting on the entrance ramp, however, a truck pulled out of a driveway and blocked the car immediately in front of me. The truck was not able to make the turn-out on the first try, and it stopped and stalled. Meanwhile, the taxi had disappeared in the distance ahead of the stalled truck. I feared our quarry was lost.

* * *

By the time the truck had re-started and got rolling up the street, we knew that the taxicab was roaring over the highway at seventy miles an hour, going wherever. It seemed hopeless but I pursued anyway. I sped onto the entrance ramp more recklessly than I had ever driven in my entire life. I pushed my car to its limit, and zipped across three lanes of traffic at over a hundred miles per hour, hoping against hope to get a glimpse of the taxi's taillights.

"Next exit!" shouted Amanda. "I know he took it!" I floored the car and zoomed over to the right to take the upcoming exit.

"He's not just riding in it, it's *his* damn taxi, isn't it?" I asked loudly, talking over the roar of my car's engine.

"I think so too!" said Amanda.

My car decelerated back onto the city streets, the anti-lock brakes pulsing noticeably as I slammed on the pedal to slow my car's descent from high speed. The unseen trail of the murderer felt fresh before us, although no taxicab was in sight.

"Let's drive," said Amanda. "Down this street. Here." And then, after a pause, "Turn here, to the left." We drove up and down several narrow avenues. Amanda looked uncertain.

"Got a scent of where he is?" I asked.

"Yes, but it's confusing. I think we've passed him. That filthy killer is here somewhere close, very close."

I made a conscious effort to drive very slowly, hoping to heighten Amanda's perceptions by driving the car more deliberately. We were in a small, very ancient part of the Barton Heights neighborhood, where a few old houses dated back to the era of Edgar Allan Poe, and one of the streets is named after him, too. The houses were mostly not restored or maintained because the neighborhood was troubled. Drug dealers ran rampant in projects just a couple of blocks away.

"He's somewhere in this area," asserted Amanda.

"It shouldn't be that hard to find a taxi driver who lives around here," I noted.

"Tomorrow, yes, that would be easy. But I think we've got to find him now. Someone's life could be in the balance." I felt her sense of urgency as well.

For long, painful minutes we drove and drove. We saw nothing other than the usual street hoodlums. Finally, something clicked in my brain. "Something wasn't right," I said. I drove back to a street where I had an odd feeling, a perception that didn't register at first in my conscious mind, but where something was clearly more wrong than usual in this run-down old neighborhood.

We were on our way to the house of the killer.

* * *

"There," I said. "Look at it."

We were stopped in front of one of the rambling, half-dilapidated great houses in Richmond's old Barton Heights neighborhood. The house had three stories and a gracious veranda, dating back over a century to a time when well-off families lived in this area. The house was built in a prosperous era, long before the neighborhood was turned over to the drug addicts and derelicts, and the poor and elderly who had no choice but to live among them.

The house was long neglected, decades overdue for paint and repair. Trash filled the yard and the porch. Attached to the house was a 1920s small garage, whose wooden gable was also unpainted. Very strangely, however, there was a brand new metal automatic garage door closed shut over the garage entrance.

The garage door was totally incongruous with the house and the neighborhood. This suburban convenience, obviously installed very recently, would not have been purchased by the poor, elderly, or under-employed families who lived on this street.

Any normal homeowner who invested in the garage door would also have done some other improvements to the house's exterior. The new garage door on this decrepit house was a signal of the unusual, and had triggered a subconscious reaction in me that made me feel something was wrong.

Amanda and I both felt a surge of emotion as we exited my car and approached the dark and suspicious old dwelling. No lights were on that we could see, and the house was quiet. We drew our guns and searched the house perimeter together. We saw nothing.

My heart was pounding with apprehension far greater than was justified by my being merely in a bad neighborhood. I felt sure this was the home of the killer, and I could see from Amanda's troubled expression that she had similar ideas. "Do you have any doubts?" I asked Amanda.

"No," she confirmed, "We're here."

We paused for a moment in the darkness. Amanda appeared to be listening for a distant sound, but I knew she was trying to feel her way to things not accessible in ordinary reality.

Amanda and I had no proof of any kind that this was the house of the killer. We had no evidence that would legally justify a search. We did not even have a basis to presume that the garage sheltered the taxicab we had been chasing.

"Do you think he's inside?" I asked her.

"Yes – yes," she nodded, confirming her own perception, "I think he's at home. And I think a woman might be about to die in there."

"Let's go," I said.

With nothing more than our hunches to back us up, we prepared to break in. We went to the back door, where I used my pocket lock-pick kit to try and jimmy open the door. I got the tumbler loose but I couldn't quite get the door open.

I used a fallen shingle to pry off the rotten door-frame. It came off easily but noisily. There was no going back now. I kicked in the door. Amanda was right behind me, her pistol also at the ready. Cold air hit us from inside, and there was a wisp of smoke that, for a moment, looked like the ghost of Uriah Jenkins.

"Motherfuck!" said a male voice in the basement of the house, and there was crashing and clanging as objects fell over, kicked by an individual quickly on the move. We heard a person of medium build quickly run up a staircase on the other side of the house.

"*Stay here, but behind the wall!*" I whispered to Amanda, while I ran over to cover the back stairs. "Police business!" I shouted loudly so I could be heard throughout the house. "Come down quietly and we'll talk."

"You'll die, motherfucker," said the voice upstairs, calm and matter-of-factly. "This .44 is all ready for you, you stupid cop piece of shit!"

A moment later there was a loud blast of odd-sounding gunfire on the side of the house where Amanda was waiting. The smell of gunpowder was also different than usual from a fired weapon.

"Amanda, are you all right?" I shouted.

"Just getting a bead here," she replied, and then I heard her own pistol fire two shots up the stairs.

I realized then what kind of gun the killer was using: It was an Old Army 19th-century-style lead ball revolver, using black powder and percussion caps. It was a strangely antique tool for a gunfight, although just as deadly as a modern weapon if properly used. Uriah Jenkins' ghost had even influenced the killer's choice of a personal defense firearm.

For a moment there was silence. Feeling the need for action, I charged up the back stairs and I ran into a blast of the killer's gun. The bullet-ball missed me, and I fired two shots of my own.

We heard the killer run down another staircase in the middle of the house, all the way down to the basement. Amanda and I met near the kitchen. We tried to turn on lights, but the wall switches didn't work.

"Jesus, all these stairs in this old house," I said. "We can't cover them all."

Just then a woman screamed, a horrible, pained, blood-chilling scream. "No, no!" she shrieked in obvious pain.

Amanda and I ran separately down two different sets of stairs. We both moved toward where we had heard the screams. Our guns were ready to shoot, but we didn't see the killer.

Downstairs, a candlelit glow came from a room at the back of the basement which contained the woman in pain, who was now crying and sobbing loudly. We burst into the room, Amanda first.

It was an old musty chamber unaltered since the last century. Candles were lit in several places. Everything in the room was old: A table and chairs, wooden boxes and tools. There was a collection of knives and cleavers and hatchets, and several whips.

Chained to the wall was a young woman. She was a pretty and thin African-American, shackled hand and foot like had been done at the slave market in the old days, or at Uriah's torture chamber at the Old Mansion. A coarse and torn dress was gathered loosely over her underwear.

She was bleeding in a number of places, her face and arms and legs and across her middle. A large bloodstain was pooling below her breasts. She had been both whipped and cut repeatedly, but she was alive. It would turn out that her wounds were not mortal.

So, even after a gunfight was underway in his own house, the killer had raced downstairs just to have the pleasure of stabbing and cutting a victim just one more time.

Amanda tended to the young woman, loosening her shackles and seeing to her wounds, while I carefully backed out of the room to hunt the killer. For a few moments I could sense no motion other than that of Amanda and the victim behind me. The killer was silently waiting.

There was a rustle in the hallway in front of me and the killer's gun fired. "Aah!" moaned Amanda behind me. She had been shot. I returned fire in front of me, but I then heard the killer race up the stairs. I bounded up after him, not knowing if Amanda was alive or dead or dying.

The killer did not try to exit his house's front door, which was closed by two time-consuming locks. He fired a shot at me as I stood at one end of a hallway, and then backed himself toward his own six-foot-long front window. I pursued and fired my gun; he fired his revolver at me. The lead bullet from his gun blew away some wall plaster behind me. I thought I had hit him as I saw his body crash through the window onto the porch in front of the house.

In fact I had hit the killer only in his weak arm, and he was not stopped. With demonic energy he practically bounced up from the wood of the porch, and he began to run. I ran to the broken window to look through the smashed glass, and I saw him go down the street and get into an old car. Some of the local street hoodlums were in between, and I did not have a clear shot against a target in motion.

I went downstairs to see if my partner was still alive. Amanda had been grazed in the shoulder by a bullet. Despite her wound, she was providing comfort to the stabbing victim, who was huddled in Amanda's arms. "We're both gonna be all right," said Amanda.

I could hear sirens in the distance, but I used the phone on the main floor to be sure ambulances were on the way. I told the 911 operator the kind of car the cops needed to find. I then returned downstairs to confer with Amanda.

"We didn't get him, did we?" she said as I returned.

"No, I thought I winged him, but he drove away. They should pick him up soon."

Amanda sat for a moment in silence. I stanched the bleeding on Amanda's wound while she attended to the bleeding abductee who had been shackled to the killer's wall.

"They *won't* find him," said Amanda with assurance. "He knows the back streets, and Uriah's ghost will shield him. He'll be long gone while the cops drive around in circles."

"He'll go to Louisa county, won't he?" I guessed.

Amanda nodded. "His home away from home," she said. "We'll find him there."

"You're going to the hospital," I said, "You and this poor girl."

"She's going, I'm not. We're going to Louisa together," she told me. "It's time to call Dabney Horton," she continued. "Call him right now, tell him briefly what happened, tell him the killer is headed for Louisa and that we'll meet Dabney there. We'll have the killer before dawn. The regular cops won't be able to find him."

I trusted Amanda's instincts as to what to do. So I got on the phone to contact the millionaire Dabney Horton who had hired us, and thus fulfilled our promise to tell *him* before even the police got the story.

I reached Dabney's secretary, who immediately patched the call through to another location where Dabney himself got on the line. Dabney listened and instantly appreciated the situation. He said he had full faith in Amanda's guess the killer would successfully escape to Louisa. I described the killer's car and what I had seen of the killer himself.

Dabney told me to meet him in Louisa county at the parking lot of the Baptist church where Amanda and I had spent that pleasant afternoon with the pastor. Dabney promised that the police would let me and Amanda go immediately after the stabbed woman was in the ambulance. He told me to have a medic verify that Amanda's wound was not dangerous to her, and urged us to head for Louisa to help the search.

As soon as I got off the phone the police and ambulances arrived. I could hear many more sirens in the distance as every available police car in Richmond began combing the streets for the serial killer whom we had discovered.

The very competent medics took charge of the stabbed young woman and rushed her to the hospital. Her wounds up to that point had been made with the specific goal of tormenting her without yet endangering her life. Aside from physical and emotional scars, she would recover.

The medics patched up Amanda and told her to come to the hospital before too many hours had passed, given her unwillingness to go there at the moment. The police commander on site briefly interviewed us while the medics were attending Amanda. He then told us he had instructions to release us to join the manhunt now spreading across central Virginia.

Amanda and I got in my car, and we headed in the same direction we felt the killer had taken.

"Why won't the police find him?" I asked Amanda. "Why couldn't the cops find an old Pontiac between here and Louisa county?"

"Uriah will shield him," she said. "He'll drive right by the cops and they will see only darkness. Uriah needs him. He'll make it to Louisa. We'll see him there."

She gently nursed her shoulder. We drove along in the car at high speed toward the countryside, but we didn't say much. I felt so indulgent toward my wounded pretty friend Amanda. I wished we didn't have to continue this chase, so I could take her to the hospital and just sit by her side.

This was now the third gunfight that Amanda and I had survived together. We were close to one another, and knew each other fairly well, but yet I found her as mystifying as ever. I wanted to talk to her but I did not know what to say, so I kept my half-formed feelings to myself as we drove along the moonlit Virginia highways.

I did feel sure, however, that the night's adventures were not complete.

Rich Man's Justice

Driving along the empty Virginia roads in the middle of the night, I felt excited and alert despite the late hour. In the evening's bright moonlight I could see that Amanda's big, dark eyes were full of energy as well, notwithstanding her minor gunshot wound. I felt privileged to be the trusted companion of this special and mystical woman.

Together we had confronted demons and the powers of death, and we were winning. Twice now I had helped to save a young woman's life, and on both occasions Amanda Poe was right there with me. We were now heading toward what we hoped would be the final capture of a serial murderer. With

Amanda, I was ready to face whatever ghosts or devils stood in our way.

As we drew close to Louisa county, Dabney Horton called us on my car phone, and I put him on the hands-free speaker.

"Good work, you two!" he said. "We've got most of the state police force as well as local police out looking for the man who shot you, Amanda. I'm a little surprised he's slipped through our fingers so far. You don't have any doubt he headed toward Louisa, do you?"

"No, Dabney, I'm sure of it," answered Amanda. "We're going to find him there," she added, with casual but unmistakable confidence.

"I can tell you a little bit about the suspect," said Dabney. "His name is Michael Blakemore, on the surface a fairly ordinary person with no criminal record. He's an only child, grew up outside Petersburg, his father died a few years ago, mother still living. He went to the University of Richmond for part of a year, then dropped out and worked at odd jobs.

"For the last half a year," Dabney continued, "he'd been employed as a taxi driver. The police think that's how he met his victims, single women alone needing a cab ride home. His taxicab was in his garage behind a new automatic garage door that he installed.

"The police found something interesting in the cab. Apparently he kept a cooler with juices and soft drinks, and in the glove box he had some sedative narcotics. He probably mixed the sedatives into some of the drinks, and gave them to selected passengers in his cab who would then fall asleep.

"Blakemore would probably then just drive the sleeping women into his garage, and then chain the poor girls to his basement wall before they awoke from the drugs. After that was torture and murder. But he's probably killed his last victim, now that you've discovered him.

"I'm at my cabin at Lake Anna now," continued Dabney. "My helicopter will get me to Louisa in a few minutes, I'll meet you there by the church. By the way, I've got your $25,000 apiece reward money with me. Soon as we catch Blakemore I'll give it to you. Amanda, we'll get you to the hospital soon, and all your medical bills are on me."

"Thanks, Dabney," said Amanda. "But we won't meet you at the church just yet. David and I are going to stay in his car and see if we can find Blakemore on our own. But we'll meet you if we don't turn anything."

"Whatever you think best," replied Dabney. "Let me know how the authorities and I can help. But remember, call me the *instant* you've got anything, that's very important. See you both shortly." Dabney signed off.

I'd actually forgotten about Dabney's reward money. That was more cash than I'd ever had in my entire life. Catching the killer and getting paid in full would indeed make it quite a night.

I felt close to success and my mood was upbeat. After we talked to Dabney, however, Amanda seemed to sink into a more dark and brooding state of mind. I thought it was an effect of her wound, but later on I would understand more about Amanda's anxieties.

* * *

As we got to Louisa county, a check with the authorities by phone confirmed that Michael Blakemore was still at large. Police cruisers were moving constantly along the Louisa by-roads, but no one had sighted Blakemore's vehicle.

"I think I know where he's going to go," said Amanda.

"Home to the Old Mansion?" I guessed. "Home to the ghost of Uriah Jenkins?"

"Yes," Amanda said. "Without having seen it before, he'll be attracted there by pure instinct."

"What would it be like," I asked, "For Michael Blakemore to spend a night in the same place where Uriah Jenkins did *his* murders in the last century? Would they be chums? Would they talk about old times, sharing murder and rape stories with each other?"

"It would be horrible," said Amanda. "Blakemore would have terrible visions and nightmares. But he would enjoy some of the terrible things he saw, and he would feel connected and close to Uriah's ghost, a bond of blood between the two of them. If he did not go completely insane, Blakemore might become even more of an evil person than before."

So it was clear where we had to go. Amanda and I had to retrace our path toward the Old Mansion where we had spent that awful night some weeks before. We turned my car onto an old, little-travelled road.

* * *

We would find the place just as we had left it a few weeks back: A few spaces for cars by some old picnic tables in a little clearing by the side of the road. A path that led away from the clearing and into the woods, an old hunter's path that ended at the stream marking the boundary of the Old Mansion grounds. Beyond that was horror from beyond the grave, horror that Amanda and I had seen firsthand.

As we drove near to the roadside clearing, my mind replayed how Amanda and I had found Uriah's ghost waiting in his 1850s home. I recalled how we found the torture chamber where young female slaves and another woman had died a horrible death. Now, in the 1990s, three young women had died a similarly horrible death in a house in Richmond.

I wondered if this was a cycle that would never end. Would there always be vicious murderers of women in every century, who once again needed to be caught and punished for their crimes? Would it always be that new killers would spring up, taking inspiration from the ghosts of criminals long dead?

There was no time now, however, for philosophical speculation. It was time to catch a killer. As we approached the area with the old picnic tables, I slowed my car down and turned out the lights. We passed the spot and saw no cars parked, no one there at all.

I made a U-turn and went back to a place I had noticed a few dozen yards down, where a small expansion of the road shoulder would allow us to park my car discreetly.

"This is the right spot to wait," said Amanda, agreeing with my thoughts. "We'll wait here for him." Amanda put her hand on my lap.

We turned off everything and waited in silence. All lights were out except that from the moon and the stars. For a good while no cars came. I got a bit drowsy.

I was suddenly startled by the sound of a horse's hooves, clip-clopping rapidly on the road beside us. The horse stopped beside the car, and the man bent over to look in the windshield. Suddenly the moon bathed his face in light, and I saw a horrible face with a mustache: It was *Uriah Jenkins*, dressed in 19th century finery and laughing hysterically. My hand gripped my pistol tightly. Uriah's face evaporated and I heard a horse gallop away.

Of course there had been no horse and no rider. We had seen the long-dead Uriah one last time.

A thick misty fog settled onto the road, making visibility almost impossible. Amanda waved her hand, and the mist began to dissipate, almost like magic. A car then came down the road. The car was an old rusty Pontiac, Michael Blakemore's car. He passed us without seeming to notice us and pulled into the clearing ahead.

I started my car and moved it forward without turning on the lights. I had my pistol in my right hand, and Amanda was holding her gun, too, both of us with safeties off. I put my car's windows down to make it easier to shoot. The night breezes suddenly became a howling wind.

We pulled into the parking area as Michael Blakemore shut off his vehicle and was getting out of it. "Police! Freeze!" I shouted above the wind, as Amanda and I both exited my car and leveled our pistols at Blakemore.

He wheeled around, drawing his own antique gun and hoping to shoot at us, but his foot caught on a rock and he fell backwards. His old-style revolver shot wildly into the trees. Amanda and I both let go some rounds from our pistols, and we blasted the door of Blakemore's auto right off of its rusty hinges. Our bullets missed Blakemore because he was already falling when we fired. Blakemore's ankle was sprained in his fall, and the car door had fallen on him, injuring his arm. Blakemore groaned loudly

I ran forward and stepped on his wrist to force him to let go of his gun. His groans turned into a scream and he let go of the pistol which Amanda moved away from him. Amanda then pointed her pistol at Blakemore's head while I moved away the car door that had dropped on his sprawled body.

His injured arm seemed numb but I put the handcuffs on him anyway. I didn't care how much he hurt. I wondered if the groaning Blakemore had any thought of comparing his own pain at the moment with that of the agonies of the women he had tortured.

"You're Michael Blakemore," I said, half-inquiring but already knowing the answer.

"I've never been here before," he said in reply, seemingly unconcerned about being arrested. "I wanted to walk through the woods."

"You wanted to find the big plantation house in your dreams," said Amanda.

"That's right, how'd you know, you bitch?" said Blakemore. "Fuck, man!" he said to me.

I had begun picking up Blakemore and shoving him into the back seat of my car. It was obvious his leg and arm were both impaired. Although he was handcuffed I took the precaution of using the safety locks to disengage the inside rear door latches.

"The Mansion, yeah," said Blakemore. "I've seen it in my sleep a hundred times, but I never knew where to find it. Somehow, tonight, I felt I could go and find it for real. Could you take me there before I go away?" he asked, seeking this favor from us.

"You'll never see it unless your ghost finds a way to go there," I said.

"Am I going to die?" he asked calmly. "Are they going to fry me in that old electric chair? Are twelve people gonna watch smoke rise from my charcoaled brain?"

"That won't be up to us," I replied.

"So you got the women knocked out with a drink," said Amanda.

"Oh, yeah," said Blakemore, seeming very talkative about his crimes. He groaned again and tried to adjust his position on the car seat, clearly bothered by the pain from his injuries. "Those girls thought I was such a nice guy, giving them a cold drink in my cab. I loved those beautiful young black girls, I dressed them up in slave costumes, and I beat them and cut them up and fucked them over and over, even after they were dead. I fucked and cut and killed a white girl, too, I didn't always discriminate."

"We know," said Amanda. "How many were there total?"

"Only three and a half so far," Blakemore answered. "A half because you two interrupted me, you assholes." He was almost whining.

It was horrible how ordinary Michael Blakemore seemed, a dweebish sort of young guy, short greasy hair, cheap clothes, a guy like one sees by the thousands in every city. Only this guy was a mass murderer.

"What happens now?" said Blakemore.

"They'll be here soon to take you away," I said. I picked up the car phone to dial Dabney Horton.

* * *

The call was put through to Horton's helicopter which was only a few miles away in the sky. Horton told us to sit tight with our prisoner and wait for him.

In about two minutes some state troopers showed up. They asked if all was secure, and looked into the back seat of my car at the handcuffed Blakemore. Surprisingly, they took no other action, but simply began to stand guard over the clearing. I began to talk to them about the capture, but the lead trooper said a special investigations team would arrive very soon, and his group was just there to provide support and security.

Dabney Horton's chopper appeared noisily overhead, flying very low. An enormously powerful searchlight shone upon us as the helicopter hovered. Then suddenly the chopper turned and darted to the side. We heard it descend to an improvised landing zone nearby.

Blakemore remained calm in the back seat of my car, just moaning intermittently in discomfort. It seemed very odd to me that the troopers did not even seek to remove Blakemore into a police vehicle. But I'd done my job; the rest was up to government personnel, and their procedures were not my concern.

I looked over at the murderer and I found there was nothing I wanted to say to him. It was the job of the police to sort out the details of his crimes. I had no desire to talk to him or inquire about his murderous passions. I simply wanted to see him taken away and receive his punishment.

Amanda looked troubled but alert. She held one hand to the shoulder where she had been wounded. I thought the look on her face was from the pain of her injury, but later I would understand the foreboding that was affecting her.

In a few minutes a large Chrysler sedan pulled up. It had fat black police car tires and lots of antennas, but it was unlike any official vehicle I had ever noticed before. Out of the car stepped two big men, obviously cops of some sort, and Dabney Horton.

The big men moved quickly to my car. They were very deliberate in their demeanor. They showed us their badges. "We're special agents with the state police," said one of them. "We know you were acting in an official capacity here, and we appreciate your assistance in the apprehension of this suspect. We'll take him into custody now."

They moved quickly into the back seat of
my Mercury, and they picked up Blakemore as
roughly as professional standards allow. "He's
injured in the arm and leg," I said, but the two
men did not respond although I know they
heard me. They hustled the moaning Blakemore
along into the Chrysler in a flash. One of the
men got in the back seat with the murderer.

The cop who joined Blakemore in the
back seat was black. I couldn't help but wonder
if this African-American cop was perhaps a
descendant of a slave who had been owned by
Colonel Horton or even Uriah Jenkins. Maybe
he even had an ancestor or distant relative who
had died in Uriah's plantation house torture
chamber.

As Blakemore was safely stowed away
with the two special officers of the state police,
Dabney Horton approached us and got in the
back seat of my car. "Let's talk for a second," he
said. He sat right where the handcuffed
murderer had been sitting.

We got in the car with Dabney, and I
turned the car key so I could roll up the
windows. "You two have done a great job," said

Dabney. "The entire Commonwealth of Virginia is in your debt." He pulled two envelopes from his inside jacket pocket. "Inside of each of these is your $25,000 reward per person, plus an additional $10,000 to cover your final expenses. I take it that's sufficient."

Not only was the money sufficient, it was extravagant almost to the point of being ridiculous. I felt like I was being bribed, but I knew as well there was nothing to do but take the money.

"That'll be it for tonight. David, I want your word of honor that you will take Amanda to the hospital *immediately* and see that she gets whatever she needs, all at my expense, of course. Okay, David?"

"Yes, definitely," I said.

"Good," replied Dabney. "There will be no more questions for you from the authorities. Just go on home. Your role in all this will be very quiet. Whatever you hear on the news, please don't react in any way. If there's any fuss, contact me directly.

"Amanda," he continued, "I'll see you again sometime. Let me know if you need anything. I want that shoulder of yours fully recovered.

"Mr. Allan," he said, turning to me, "It was good to meet with you and benefit from your services. Thank you once again." Dabney Horton then shook our hands and departed. He rode away in the car with the murderer in it, joining the other state police agent in the front seat.

The other state police cruisers drove away as well, no one else saying a word to us.

"That was strange," I said. "No questions, no reports, no one asking us anything about what the killer said or did. Those two special agents just grabbed Blakemore and disappeared in a hurry with Dabney. They didn't even read him his rights. What do you think is going on?" I asked Amanda.

"Can you follow that Chrysler at long distance, without them knowing?" asked Amanda.

"Out here in the country it should be easy," I said. We got in my car and buckled the seat belts.

I put my vehicle in gear and turned on just the parking lights. We followed the direction of the Chrysler, but I remained well back, purposefully losing sight of the car around bends in the road, in places where I knew I could quickly catch up.

The sedan with Dabney Horton and the murderer was not heading back toward Richmond, nor toward the Louisa county jail. It also was not heading toward the highway and the nearest state police office.

"Where are they going?" I said.

"Let's not lose them," answered Amanda.

* * *

A few miles further and the Chrysler slowed onto the shoulder; it stopped and its lights went out. There was a four-wheel-drive Range Rover parked just ahead of it. I turned off my own car's lights and paused well back to observe.

In the moonlight I saw one figure move from the Chrysler to the Range Rover. The Range Rover's lights came on, and I saw two men hustle a third into the vehicle. The Range Rover turned off into the woods.

I turned my car's parking lights back on, and drove up to the Chrysler, now parked and empty. The Range Rover's taillights were slowly disappearing up a difficult narrow path into the woods. "My car would never make it through there," I said to Amanda.

"I see," she said. "We can't follow them. But drive a little further on the paved road, and then take the next right."

"Okay," I said, and did as she asked.

"David, do you know what's at the end of that path through the woods?"

"No."

"The Pataquoy River," said Amanda. All of a sudden I felt sick. Now I knew what was going on. The riverbank of the Pataquoy was the site of the big hanging-tree where, in 1859, Colonel Horton had hanged Uriah Jenkins. I could never forget spending the night there with Amanda, and re-living the secret vigilante execution carried out under the direction of Dabney Horton's ancestor.

I knew now that Dabney Horton was taking the serial murderer Michael Blakemore out to that same tree.

Some hundreds of feet up ahead, the Pataquoy River curved toward the road on which we were driving. There was an old railroad bridge crossing the river there, from a long-abandoned line of the Virginian Railway.

Amanda and I parked the car by the side of the road where we could see the remainder of the old train tracks. We walked out onto the bridge that spanned the moonlit river, carefully stepping from one railroad tie onto another. The stars and moon were bright, but the wind was cold and howling.

We got to a spot on the bridge where we could easily see down river, to a clearing where a large ancient tree pointed its stout limb toward the water.

Four men stood there by the tree, seemingly talking. Amanda and I were silent. We knew a hanging was about to take place, a secret hanging, a hanging that no one would ever admit to having performed, a hanging that Amanda and I could never disclose to public or police. After all, who would ever believe that respected millionaire Dabney Horton would ever hang a man by the side of a Virginia river, aided and abetted by the state police?

Amanda and I had our handguns, and we could shoot that distance, but not with enough accuracy. Our bullets might miss everyone, or kill any one or two of those four men. The fact was, there was nothing we could reasonably do. Moreover, although it was lynch justice, it was a form of justice nonetheless, a justice that might be truer than what could result from the courts.

If Michael Blakemore went to court, there would be questions, legalities, technicalities, pleas, objections. The whole manner of how he was captured was legally questionable, considering the way we had broken into his house. Not to mention our unofficial status on the case, working with police credentials but actually being paid by Dabney Horton.

Michael Blakemore, as a man who cut up women in his basement, could plead insanity and win. Obviously only crazy people cut up young women in their cellars, so he had a good start on an insanity defense.

357

But our thoughts didn't matter to the men about to execute Michael Blakemore. Amanda and I watched as three men hauled a rope down from a tree limb, a rope that was weighted at its other end with a human body, a human who was slightly injured but very much alive as the noose tightened around his neck. His legs kicked wildly under him as he died slowly in the noose, three men watching stolidly below him as his eyes bulged and tongue swelled in the hanging death which, for many centuries, has been the classic fate of rapists and killers.

After many minutes, the legs stopped swinging, the body stopped swaying. The body was then jolted by a single final gunshot blast into the heart of the suspended corpse, to make certain the execution was complete.

Michael Blakemore, serial murderer of young and mostly black women, was dead, his ghost now joining that of Uriah Jenkins' in murderers' hell. Michael Blakemore had been hung by the neck until dead in the exact spot his ghostly role-model had been hung more than a century earlier.

Amanda and I went back to our car in silence. As we reached the place where the railroad tracks stopped due to being paved over by the road, Amanda shared with me one last vision she had about this case.

"They are throwing his body in the same secret ditch where they moved Uriah Jenkins' bones the other week, after we threatened to expose the Horton family secret. The two killers are going to be buried there forever. Uriah Jenkins will not affect this world anymore, but there is another ghost from a hanged corpse to cause trouble in his place."

We drove home in an unhappy quiet. I took Amanda to a hospital near our homes in Richmond, a city now free of a serial killer of young women.

We had done our part in finding this criminal and preventing him from ever killing and raping again. It was good, in one sense, that the murderer Michael Blakemore was dead.

But Amanda and I both knew that justice is better served by truth for the whole community, than by private actions oriented to the egos of a few powerful people and the protection of their wealth and status.

* * *

The next day in the news they said that suspected serial killer Michael Blakemore had been shot in a gunfight in his home, and that he made it to Louisa county where he was shot a second time in the heart and fell into the Pataquoy River. It was a lie, but it was enough of a story to put the fears of citizens to rest.

Amanda and I knew the real truth about the end of this murderer, just like we knew the truth about another Virginia murderer in the century before, but these were truths we needed to keep to ourselves for a while yet to come.

More of Amanda Poe

Amanda Poe and her partner may be seen again in more titles to come of the mystical Amanda Poe Mysteries.